Feet in Chains

Feet in Chains

Kate Roberts

Translated from the Welsh
by Katie Gramich

Parthian, Cardigan SA43 1ED
www.parthianbooks.com
First published in Welsh as *Traed Mewn Cyffion* in 1936
This edition published 2020
© Estate of Kate Roberts
Translation © Katie Gramich 2012
ISBN 978-1-908069-56-6
Cover image: A detail from the linocut series Rhosgadfan by Sir Kyffin
Williams with kind permission of Gwasg Gregynog
Typeset by Claire Houguez
Printed by 4edge Limited
Printed and bound by 4edge Limited, UK
Published with the financial support of the Books Council of Wales
British Library Cataloguing in Publication Data
A cataloguing record for this book is available from the British Library.

I Johannes, Eluned a Gwyneth

Introduction

Kate Roberts

Kate Roberts (1891-1985) was the most important Welsh female novelist and short story writer of the twentieth century. From 1918 to the early 1980s she produced an impressive body of literary work, including eighteen volumes of creative prose, extensive political journalism, a number of plays, many critical essays, and a voluminous and fascinating correspondence. In addition to being a writer, she was a political activist and one of the first and most industrious members of Plaid Genedlaethol Cymru, the Welsh Nationalist Party, founded in 1925, as well as an impassioned and successful campaigner for Welsh-medium education.

Katherine Roberts was born in 1891 in the small Caernarfonshire village of Rhosgadfan, which is lightly fictionalised as 'Moel Arian' in the novel, *Feet in Chains*. The eldest of what would be the four children of Catrin and Owen Roberts, a quarryman and smallholder, she had three younger brothers: Richard, Evan, and David. Their cottage, which is still extant, was called 'Cae'r Gors', meaning 'the field of the marsh', and the name is an accurate indication of the landscape surrounding it: this is upland north-west Wales, not far from the massive peaks of Snowdonia.

Roberts won a scholarship to the County School in Caernarfon in 1904 and went on in 1910 to study at the

University College of North Wales, Bangor, where she was one of a very small number of female students at the time. She was acutely aware of her privilege and of the financial sacrifice her education meant for her parents. She studied Welsh, although, according to the Anglicizing educational policies of the time, all her lectures were ironically through the medium of English. Nevertheless, the Welsh Society at Bangor was lively and the young Kate Roberts was at the heart of its various cultural and social activities: eisteddfods, debates, and student newspapers.

She left Bangor in 1913 with a degree in Welsh and a teacher's certificate. She took a post as a Primary School teacher in Llanberis for a year; her salary here was only £60 a year, and she was unable to teach her own specialism, leaving her feeling frustrated, much like the character, Twm, in *Feet in Chains*. In February 1915, though, she took up a teaching post at a Secondary School in Ystalyfera in the Swansea Valley, which had become vacant owing to a male teacher leaving to go to War. The move to south Wales was quite a wrench for Roberts and at first she found it hard to understand the unfamiliar dialect, but this was the beginning of a twenty-year period of 'exile' in south Wales for Roberts and, although her homesickness for Caernarfonshire was powerful at times, it is clear that she profited from her different experience there. It is as well to remember that *Feet in Chains*, though redolent of Snowdonia, was actually written in the industrialized valleys of South Wales.

Forming a close friendship with two other women teachers, Betty Eynon Davies and Margaret Price, Kate Roberts began collaborating with them writing plays, which they also performed up and down the Tawe valley during the War. Kate Roberts' brothers were by now soldiers in the British Army, their lives in imminent danger. The intense worry of this period is rendered in *Feet in Chains*, when Twm joins up and his parents anxiously await his letters.

After cutting her teeth as a writer in collaborative drama, Roberts began writing short stories at the end of the War. She said in interviews that what precipitated her writing was the death in the war of her youngest brother, David, in 1917, and the traumatic grief of that loss. She saw writing as a therapeutic activity, feeling that she needed to write or choke with anger and indignation. She asserted in her 1960 autobiography, *Y Lôn Wen* (*The White Lane*), that 'everything important, everything that made a deep impression, happened to me before 1917'.[1] And yet 1917 is, somewhat paradoxically, 'Year 1' in the history of Kate Roberts the fiction writer.

In 1925 her first volume of short stories, *O Gors y Bryniau* (*From the Marsh in the Hills*) was published. These early stories are rooted in a particular place, the upland Caernarfonshire landscape of her childhood. The characters and events of the stories are very much shaped by the place, a close-knit, Welsh-speaking community of smallholders and quarry-workers much like that in which Roberts herself grew up. But her work is far from being parochial. It is geographically specific, yet it speaks of a common early twentieth-century feeling of cultural anxiety and 'things falling apart', charting shifts in family and gender roles, and expressing a longing for what is past simultaneously with an overwhelming desire for change.

By the end of 1917 she had moved to a post in the Girls' County School in Aberdare, where she became a prominent member of the Cymmrodorion Society, rising to president by 1925. Yet her energetic community activity was soon to be channelled in a different, more political, direction. Plaid Genedlaethol Cymru (the Welsh Nationalist Party) was founded in 1925 and at first Kate Roberts, an instinctive socialist, was reluctant to join, but by 1926 she had not only become a member but found herself Chair of the Women's Committee. Joining the party signalled a decisive step in Roberts' life as a political campaigner and journalist, but it also had directly personal consequences, for it was in the first Plaid summer School in Machynlleth in 1926 that she met Morris T. Williams, a young man ten years her junior, whom she would marry within two years.

Marriage at the age of 37 had immediate professional consequences for Kate Roberts. Due to the legal bar in place against the employment of married women as teachers at the time, she had to relinquish her post in Aberdare, and the newly-married couple moved to Rhiwbina in Cardiff in January 1929. Kate Roberts and her husband became dedicated political campaigners, united in their work for Plaid Genedlaethol Cymru, as well as sharing literary interests and ambitions. Freed from the burdens of teaching, Roberts continued to publish volumes of short stories, which show her gradual mastery of the form.

From Rhiwbina, Kate Roberts and her husband moved to Tonypandy in the Rhondda Valley in the summer of 1931. Roberts gained a first-hand view of the poverty of the Rhondda during the Depression: the many families living in a single house, the lack of food and clothing and, an important point for Kate Roberts, these people's general lack of the Welsh language and their ignorance of its culture. In 1933-4 when she was writing the novel *Feet in Chains* she was being taken back in her memory and imagination to the north Wales of her youth, but it is clear that Roberts was very much concerned by the hardship of the people of the Rhondda on her doorstep. While Kate Roberts herself came from a poor background, in the early 1930s she and her husband must have counted themselves relatively well off in comparison with their neighbours in Tonypandy.

In 1935, though, the novel completed and a winner in the 1934 National Eisteddfod, Kate Roberts and Morris T. Williams decided to move back to north Wales and to take on a new venture. Williams was a master printer by trade, so it made sense for them to become partners in this major project: the buying and running of Gwasg Gee, a well-known publishing house, in Denbigh. This meant a move back to their native north Wales for both. For Kate Roberts the creative writer, though, this move was the beginning of a period of creative silence, as she dedicated her formidable energies firstly to making the press a successful business and, secondly, to writing for *Baner ac Amserau Cymru* (*The Banner and Times of Wales*), the newspaper which they took over at Gwasg Gee in the late 1930s. For a while, Kate Roberts the short story writer, novelist and playwright was transformed into Kate Roberts the businesswoman and journalist. When her husband died suddenly and unexpectedly in 1946, though, the second, lengthy period of Roberts' life as a writer of fiction began. From the late forties until her death in 1985, she would go on to publish two further novels, two novellas, an autobiography, and six volumes of short stories. By the time of her death she was widely recognized in Wales as 'the queen of our literature'.

Feet in Chains

Kate Roberts wrote her novel *Feet in Chains* in the early 1930s while she was living in 7 Kenry Street, Tonypandy, in the Rhondda Valley. Although the novel is set in the north-west corner of Wales, in the foothills of Snowdonia, where Kate Roberts was born and spent her childhood, and deals with the period from 1880 to 1917, the bleak vision of the novel is surely influenced by the dire economic situation of the South Wales Valleys during the Depression. In a letter written to her friend, the poet and novelist Saunders Lewis, in December 1933, Roberts mentions working on the novel but gives much more space to the material conditions of life in Tonypandy: she tells Lewis about donating clothes and money collected in Bala and Aberystwyth to a Salvation Army officer to distribute to the needy. She explains that:

> The Salvation Army here give breakfast four times a week to two hundred children for 2d each, and twenty volunteers get up at 5.30 to go and prepare it. Last Friday there was a hullabuloo in one corner: a boy caught stealing some bread and margarine to take home. When the Major confronted him, he said that he was taking the food home to his mother because she was starving. She promised to call by to see the mother, and I haven't heard yet whether it was a true story or not. But the Major told me that this is the poorest place she's ever been in and she has twenty-five years' experience of working with the Salvation Army. I'd like to knock some of these facts into the skulls of most members of the Central Committee of Plaid Cymru.[2]

Economic imperatives were thus uppermost in Roberts' mind at this time, and she focuses unremittingly on the savage economic conditions of the lives of the characters in her novel. In fact, when Saunders Lewis read the first draft, under its original title of 'Suntur a Chlai' ['Soil and Clay'] he complained that the characters lived a monotonously materialist life, and had no spiritual dimension whatsoever.[3] He goes as far as to suggest that 'it is because you refuse to examine questioningly and deeply their religious lives that the novel is a failure.'[4] This elicited a furious response from the very thin-skinned Kate Roberts, who replied immediately:

> If I were to set about writing a novel about religious life I would do so as an atheist and I would attack religion in all its forms. My soul detests Christianity. I love some Christians but as for religion, I think it's responsible for the fact that the world is in the state it is today, and it has supported hypocritical capitalists over the centuries since the times of the early Church.[5]

Clearly, Roberts is being deliberately inflammatory here, since she is addressing a devout Catholic convert, and it is also true to say that at other stages of her life she adopted a much more conciliatory and even positive attitude towards religion. Nevertheless, this is the Kate Roberts of the mid-1930s, living in the midst of appalling deprivation, fighting hard to try to open the eyes of her fellow nationalists to harsh economic facts. It is no wonder that Roberts in due course changed the title of her novel from the quasi-Biblical 'Soil and Clay' to the more politically radical *Feet in Chains*, with its inevitable echoes of both Rousseau and Marx.[6]

It is notable that in this novel Roberts is implicitly challenging the stereotype of the Welsh as a religious, Nonconformist people, which had held sway since the late nineteenth century. Certainly she shows the chapel as an important social and cultural institution in the community of Moel Arian, but Saunders Lewis is accurate when he says that her characters lack a spiritual dimension. They attend chapel regularly, but Kate Roberts reveals this practice for what it is: a conforming to social convention and habit. Yet socialism does not appear to be the answer either. She dispatches William in the novel to the South when he becomes a socialist – it seems that socialism can't sink its roots deeply into the thin soil of Snowdonia. Nevertheless, William's impassioned belief in the injustice of the present system is implicitly shared by the authorial voice of the novel. By its end, even the placid character, Owen, is convinced of the 'possibility of doing something, instead of suffering mutely. It was high time for someone to stand up against all this injustice. To do something. Thinking about it, that was the trouble with his people. They were heroic in their capacity to suffer, and not in their capacity to do something to oppose the cause of their suffering' (*Feet in Chains*, Chapter 25). Kate Roberts' novel, then, though it is set in the recent past, can be said to engage directly with the political crisis of the 1930s and in this regard can be compared with other politically-engaged texts emerging from the South Wales valleys in the period, such as Lewis Jones's classic Communist novel, *Cwmardy* (1937), though it differs from them in its female-centredness.

Although Roberts was both a political activist and a creative writer, she very carefully steered a path away from propaganda. Her essays and correspondence show that she was both widely read and intensely interested in questions of aesthetics and style. She was an admirer of the fiction of James Joyce but realized that she could not follow either his artistic path into exile or that of the committed Communist writer Lewis Jones, who had relatively little regard for aesthetics. She admitted, somewhat ruefully perhaps, that, unlike Joyce's Stephen Dedalus and indeed Joyce himself, she did not feel the need to 'fly by the nets' of nationality, language and religion.[7] Nor did she devote her literary skills to Modernist experimentation, though she admired it in the work of Joyce and, especially, of Virginia Woolf. Instead, she adopted a rigorously realist mode of expression in order to give the Welsh world she created an unmistakeable air of authenticity. She conjured it into being in her native tongue, Welsh, and chronicled the lives of hardship struggled through by 'her' people. Francesca Rhydderch has called Roberts' style 'a politically rigorous anti-modernis[m], rather than a provincially unfashionable realis[m]'.[8] Her decision to adopt a realist mode, then, can be seen as a deliberate choice, suggestive of her determination to plough her own furrow, both stylistically and ideologically. And this she continued to do, admirably, for the rest of her long and prolific career as a writer.

Notes

1 'Digwyddasai popeth pwysig i mi cyn 1917, popeth dwfn ei argraff.' See Kate Roberts, *Y Lôn Wen* (Denbigh: Gee, 1960), p. 30. For a parallel text translation of this work, see Gillian Clarke, *The White Lane* (Llandysul: Gomer, 2009), p. 22.

2 Kate Roberts, Letter to Saunders Lewis, 12 December 1933, in *Annwyl Kate, Annwyl Saunders, Gohebiaeth 1923-1983* [*Dear Kate, Dear Saunders, Correspondence 1923-1983*], ed. Dafydd Ifans (Aberystwyth: National Library of Wales, 1992), p. 103. My translation. All further translations from the Welsh are mine unless otherwise stated.

3 Letter from Saunders Lewis to Kate Roberts, Christmas 1934, ibid. p. 108.

4 Ibid. p. 109.

5 Letter from Kate Roberts to Saunders Lewis, 28 December 1934, ibid. p. 110.

6 The arresting opening sentence of Jean-Jacques Rousseau's seminal work of political theory, *The Social Contract* (1762) are 'Man was born free, and he is everywhere in chains'. Similarly, Karl Marx and Friedrich Engels conclude the Communist Manifesto of 1848 with the words: 'The workers have nothing to lose but their chains. They have a world to win. Workers of the world, unite!'

7 'I never escaped. Never wanted to escape', cited in Emyr Humphreys, *The Triple Net: A Portrait of the Writer Kate Roberts* (London: Channel 4, 1988), p. 3.

8 Francesca Rhydderch, 'Cultural translations: a comparative critical study of Kate Roberts and Virginia Woolf', Ph.D., Wales, Aberystwyth, 2001, p. 104.

Feet in Chains

Thou prevailest forever against him, and he passeth:
thou changest his countenance, and sendest him away.
His sons come to honour, and he knoweth it not;
and they are brought low, but he perceiveth it not of them.

Job 14: 20-21

1

The humming of insects, the seedpods of the gorse cracking, heat rising hazily, and the velvety voice of the preacher murmuring on and on. If they hadn't been out in the open air it would have felt stifling, and more than half the congregation would have fallen asleep. This was the Sunday in June when the Methodists of Moel Arian held their prayer meeting. Since the chapel was small and the attraction of prayer meetings in 1880 a powerful one, it was held out in a field. The preacher was borne onward by the tide of his own eloquence. Everything was in his favour: a large crowd before him; warm, calm weather; the dome of the sky above far off and blue; the sea itself blue all the way to the horizon; and a circle of mountains as a backdrop. He had both nature and the people for his audience, and he was able to sail through his sermon with nothing to bar his way or restrict his breath, except his tight collar and starched suit. He himself was more dignified than his pulpit, which was a cart with its shafts sticking up. But even in a chapel he would surely have commanded the attention of the whole congregation, since there was something attractive about his face, with its Roman nose and clean-shaven upper lip; his mild, blue eyes; his wavy red hair and his long sideburns. As it was, many eyes were upon him, the eyes of those at the front of the crowd; but there was discontent at the edges, especially among the women, whose new shoes were pinching, their new stays too tight, and the high collars of their new frocks suffocating. They mopped the sweat from their faces and shuffled their feet irritably.

One of these women was Jane Gruffydd, who had recently married Ifan, the son of Y Fawnog. For some time now she had been almost groaning in her desire to go home. Her waist was one of the smallest among the women in the congregation, as a result of much tugging at the cords of her stays before she started her way to the service. Her bustle was the largest in the field, the satin of her dress was the heaviest and stiffest there; it was she who had the most frills on her frock and the heaviest feather on her hat. Many of the women's eyes were upon her, since very few of them owned a satin dress which could stand up on its own. The best they could afford was French merino, and a gold chain to hang from a button on their bodice was quite beyond them. Many looked at Jane Gruffydd with a curiosity greater than that attracted by her clothes alone, for Ifan Y Fawnog had gone to the far end of Lleyn to find a wife. She was tall, and wore her clothes well. She was not beautiful apart from her hair, which was arranged today low down on the nape of her neck, but there was strength in her face. Jane knew that, as a stranger who was also a newly-wed, she was being examined carefully, and if it were for that reason alone, she prayed for the preacher to finish. She could feel her armpits dripping with sweat and worried about the damage being done to her dress. But the preacher just went on and on, his voice having risen to a new pitch of excitement by this time.

She was not used to long sermons, since she had been a churchgoer before her marriage. She would be bound to faint in a minute if the man did not shut up, and the women of the congregation would of course interpret that in their own way, and perhaps they would be right, too. But, thank goodness, now he was finishing, and when the congregation started to sing, she was able to tell Ifan to bring his friends back for a cup of tea, as she was going to dash home to put the kettle on the fire. She picked her way quickly through the farmyard, pulling on the braid that she wore around her waist and in this way raising the train of her skirt out of the dirt. When she reached the house she took off her clothes and lay down on the bed, stretching out luxuriously in sheer pleasure at the feeling of release. Then she put on her everyday stays, her work bodice and skirt and a white apron on top. Thankfully, she had started preparing the tea before she had left for the prayer meeting.

The table was crammed with people drinking tea, people who had come from far away to attend the prayer meeting, and Jane was in her element. The house, with its old dresser, its clock which she'd had from her mother, and its old oak chairs, was burnished to a high shine, and the food was good. She was so glad that she had enough of those up-to-date little glass plates to give to each of the strangers to hold their cake and jam. She glanced at Ifan from time to time; he wasn't exactly in his element. Yet he had been fine a short while ago, enjoying the sermon, when she had looked at him in admiration, wearing his black

7

jacket and waistcoat and his pinstripe trousers. But now he seemed crestfallen, and he frowned whenever a little woman they called Dolly spoke. Jane didn't know any of the people, but she tried to be welcoming since they were people whom Ifan had wanted to have to tea. There must be something wrong with Ifan or he wouldn't be so silent with his friends. Perhaps he was in a bad mood because she had run off home before the end. Well, what's done is done, never mind. This Dolly spoke more than anyone else, and as she waited for her tea she stared at every corner of the kitchen, and when Jane rose to put water in the teapot Dolly's eyes followed every line of her body. Every time she said anything complimentary, there was a mocking half-smile on her lips, such as when she said about the plates,

'You certainly live in style here.'

And then in the bedroom as she was putting on her hat before going out to the evening service:

'Dear me, you do have a smart place, a washstand and a dressing-table and everything.'

'Mam gave me these.'

They were mahogany tables, and the washstand had a white marble top.

As they had arranged beforehand, Jane did not go to the chapel that evening, and as Ifan set off with the visitors, he turned a half-imploring, half-apologetic gaze on his wife. She thought how handsome he looked in his wedding suit.

The cows dragged themselves slowly towards the cowshed. They licked up their coarse oats and India corn greedily as the halters were tied around their necks, and they dozed on their feet after they finished. Jane sat on a stool, her head leaning gently on the cow's belly, gazing out towards the sea. Everywhere was silent, and there was contentment in her eyes as she looked down over the quiet, level surface of the sea. And yet she did not feel entirely content. She thought about the tea table. Something was wrong. Then she thought about the quarryman's clothes to be washed tomorrow, work which was unfamiliar to her.

She drove the cattle back to the field. They were reluctant to put one hoof in front of the other. Jane tried to make them hurry up by placing her hand on the last one's rump and pushing. The sun went down over the sea behind them, and the shadows of herself and the cattle were thrown in front of them, making it seem as if the cattle would go on and on forever. One of them was heavy with calf, and had difficulty getting through the gap. The water falling from the spout into the pool was a hard, clear sound in the silence of the night. There was no sign of life anywhere, except for an occasional man seen out for a walk carrying a baby in a shawl, while his wife was in chapel, and the occasional sick man sitting in a doorway.

Ifan came home early, having escaped before the evening prayer meeting and before Jane could say a word, he burst out,

'Can you ever forgive me, Jane?'

'What for, for goodness' sake?'

'For letting that Dolly come here to tea.'

'Why, wasn't she supposed to come?'

'No she wasn't,' and he banged the arm of his chair with his fist; 'she snuck in here after Bob Owen; people think they can do such things during prayer meetings. I didn't ask her at all. The shameless bitch, making me say such a thing after such a good sermon.'

'Well, to be honest, I didn't like her. She was praising everything too much in a spiteful way.'

At that point, Ifan managed to explain that this was Dolly Rhyd Garreg, whom he'd courted and thought of marrying at one time. But when his father was killed in the quarry, and the responsibilities of the head of the household fell upon him, since he was the oldest of the children who still remained unmarried, he had had to postpone thoughts of marriage. Dolly had become impatient with waiting, and started going around with other men. He finished with her then.

'I see now why she wanted to come here to tea,' said his wife. 'I'm glad I brought out all my best things to put on the table.'

2

On the Monday morning after the prayer meeting, Sioned Gruffydd, Ifan's mother, saw fit to go and visit her daughter-in-law in Ffridd Felen. She had Geini, her daughter, to do her laundry, and she didn't care a jot how much trouble her presence would cause in anyone's house on a washday. She would have to visit her daughter-in-law sometime, and Monday morning was as good a time as any in Sioned Gruffydd's opinion. She probably wouldn't have much to say to Jane, though the prayer meeting the previous day would give them something to talk about, at any rate.

Meanwhile Jane was busy scouring Ifan's work-clothes on an old table, out beside the water-pump. She was working hard scrubbing at the corduroy trousers, from which the water of the first wash was seeping, thick and grey. She used the back of the hand which was brandishing the scrubbing brush to wipe away the sweat from her forehead and to push back strands of hair which had fallen forward over her face. The cloth jacket was boiling away on the fireplace in the house.

'Hey,' came a voice from the direction of the house,

and she rushed to see who was there. Her heart sank when she saw that it was her mother-in-law. She disliked the thought of getting to know her mother-in-law, and she liked it even less when she wanted to get on with her work.

'Don't let me disturb you,' said Sioned Gruffydd, 'I'll just settle myself down by here,' and she sat down on a rock close by the fountain.

Jane didn't want to do work which was unfamiliar to her, such as scouring clothes, under the judgmental gaze of her mother-in-law.

'No, I'll come inside now,' said Jane, 'I was about to have a cup of tea myself after putting these trousers on to boil.'

And she took the trousers off the board, rinsed them in a clean bucket under the fountain, and then carried them to the house.

'Washing a quarryman's clothes is heavy work,' said Sioned Gruffydd.

'Yes, but I'll get used to it,' Jane replied.

'I don't know; you'll find that washing a quarryman's clothes is something you never get used to.'

'Well, I wasn't used to any kind of work when I was eight years old, but when I was eighteen I was, and I'll soon get used to this too.'

'And there'll be more and more clothes to wash as you get older,' suggested the mother-in-law.

'And perhaps I'll have some girls to help me with it then,' countered the daughter.

Jane had tried to hold her tongue as best she could, but she was unable to, for she had heard nothing of her mother-in-law up to now and she saw nothing appealing or attractive in her at this moment.

Jane put the trousers in the pan. She moved the pan to

the side of the fire and put the kettle in its place. She had nothing but bread, butter, and cheese to offer her visitor.

'How did you like the sermon yesterday?' asked Sioned Gruffydd, changing the subject.

'It was fine, as far as I could tell, though it was much too long for such a hot afternoon.'

'Well, yes, for someone with such a tiny waist, it must have been very painful to be standing around for so long.'

'I noticed that the men were looking just as bored as the women.'

'Of course, you're not used to such long sermons in the church.'

'No, but we're used to standing for ages.'

'Are you planning to go to church or to chapel?'

'That depends on how I like the church here. It's far away, but if I like it, I won't mind the distance.'

'I don't think Ifan would like you going to the church.'

'Ifan and I talked these things over before we got married, and he doesn't mind where I go.'

'His father would be shocked to hear him say such a thing.'

'Was Ifan's father a devout chapelgoer then?'

'Yes, he certainly was. He was one of the first to talk about building a chapel up here. He would find it very strange to think that any member of his family would pass by the chapel to go to church.'

'Isn't it a good thing that the dead can't think anything at all?'

Sioned Gruffydd pretended to be shocked at such blasphemy.

'I heard that you had a big crowd here for tea yesterday.'

'Yes.'

13

'Geini was sure that she would be invited.'

'Well, why didn't she come, then? She would have been very welcome. I left the sermon sooner than the rest, and left it to Ifan to invite whoever he wanted to bring with him.'

'Dolly Rhyd Garreg was here, wasn't she?'

'Yes, but she came without being invited.'

'Yes. She probably feels quite bold when it comes to Ifan.'

'Ifan had no desire to see her.'

'There's no need for him to be like that. Dolly's a fine woman.'

Jane felt all the indignation within her rising to the surface.

'Yes, she was very fine for you, allowing you to keep hold of Ifan for so long.'

'That was lucky for you.'

'I don't deny that, but you can't deny that it was even luckier for you.'

'I don't know; perhaps it would have been better for Ifan to get married when he was younger.'

'Perhaps it would have been better for Dolly, or for some other woman, but not for you, nor me.'

'Dolly would have made him a good wife.'

'And Ifan would have made her a good husband, but he was a better son to you.'

Jane said this with perfect self-possession, and Sioned Gruffydd was silenced.

After she had gone, Jane felt angry with herself for answering her mother-in-law back so harshly on her first visit. But she consoled herself with the thought that she had been sorely goaded into it. She didn't care at all about being rude to Sioned Gruffydd, but she was anxious at the thought that Ifan might be hurt if he got to hear of it.

She replaced the pan of washing on the fire, and set about cleaning the kitchen while the clothes were boiling. She took them out again to the fountain, and again someone called out 'Hey!' It was Geini, Ifan's sister, this time, and Jane was startled.

'Don't worry,' said Geini 'you must be quite fed up with seeing members of our family today. I just dashed down in case Mam had been unkind to you.'

'I'm afraid that it was me who was unkind to your mother,' said Jane.

'About time someone put her in her place; but let's see, I'll finish off this washing for you. Let me borrow your heavy apron a minute.'

And, grabbing the scrubbing brush, she set to work on the clothes with her strong, naked arms.

'I'll just pop up to the house, then, and make us a couple of pancakes for tea,' said Jane.

In half an hour Jane came to call Geini to tea, as she was pegging out the washing on the line in the field.

'You mustn't take any notice of Mam,' Geini said, 'I can just imagine what she said to you this morning. She's not angry with you but angry with Ifan for marrying at all. You see, Mam's a woman who needs a man to take care of her all the time, and when father was killed, Ifan filled the gap all too well.'

'It's a shame that he got married at all, then.'

'Not at all; Mam had Ifan for long enough to save money at his expense, and all the other children were able to run free, without offering to help at all. It'll do Mam a world of good to be left to her own devices.'

'What annoyed me most,' said Jane, 'was hearing her

sing the praises of that Dolly.'

'Mam singing Dolly's praises!' Geini laughed out loud. 'I never heard such a thing. She never had a good word to say about her until she married that little Steward. But don't take any notice of Mam; I think, to judge by the look on her face this morning, that you did the best thing you could have done for her. She's realized that she's met her match in you. She'll leave you alone now. Anyway, these pancakes are delicious.'

'Here, there are plenty more – have another; I put cream from the top of the milk in the mixture.'

And the soft pancakes smothered in butter slithered off the fork onto Geini's plate.

'Look', said Geini as she left, 'we'll have to go and see Grandmother one day. I'm sure you'll like her.'

3

It was a hot day in late June when Jane and Geini crossed the Waun Goch in the direction of Allt Eilian to visit Geini's grandmother, her father's mother. They made their way over sheep tracks, among the gorse and heather bushes. Sometimes the hems of their long skirts caught in a branch of gorse, and as they tugged their skirts away, it pricked their legs. The heat danced in front of their eyes like a cloud of insects. They could hear the sound of stones tumbling down the quarry's tip, and in the distance they heard the explosions in Llanberis like a far-off revolution. A wide expanse of land lay in front of them and behind them, and stretching away to their left was the sea.

Jane turned her gaze back all the time towards the Eifl, and she felt a pang of homesickness as she thought of her old home beyond those peaks. The landscape around her was utterly alien. She did not come from a place of explosions and rubble tips. Over there beyond the Eifl was a land of substantial farms and houses far-flung from one another, which might look cold and unneighbourly at first glance but which were really welcoming and friendly to those who knew them. And here she was, Jane Sarn Goch, among strangers, in a land where the houses were much closer together but less welcoming to her. What were her mother and father doing now, she wondered? Having tea, probably.

'Do you feel homesick?' said Geini, seeing her turn to gaze into the distance for perhaps the fifth time.

'I get a few pangs of homesickness sometimes,' she said, 'just a feeling that I'd like to pop over for a visit, and then rush back again. I'll get over it in time.'

'Don't fret, we'll have a bit of fun with Grandma; she comes from Lleyn originally too.'

Jane immediately felt better.

Betsan Gruffydd was sitting by the fireplace in that expectant way that old people have, that sense of waiting for nothing at all. Geini went straight in, calling, 'Is there anyone at home?'

And a voice came from the corner: 'Who's there?'

The old woman shaded her eyes with her hand, to deflect the sunlight flooding in from the window.

'Oh, Geini, it's you, and who's this other woman you've got with you?'

'It's Jane, Ifan's wife, who's come to see you.'

'And how are you, my girl?' said the old woman, extending her hand. 'Sit down,' and she surrendered her chair, which was in the shape of a half-circle, to Jane.

The old woman was wearing a woollen petticoat, with a bodice over the top, and a blue and white apron. She had a white cap on her head, with a lace frill around the edge. The cap was tied under her chin, and on top she wore a little round black hat. Between the ties of her cap and her woven shawl you could see the loose skin of

18

her neck dangling down. Around her was her furniture of dark oak – a dresser, a clock and a two-part sideboard, and a brass skillet hanging on the side of the dresser, which was full of old-fashioned crockery. On the walls hung family portraits from different eras.

'Geini,' said the old woman, 'pour a drop of water in this kettle, will you?'

Then she gave the fire a poke and put more dried cowdung on it, until a flame broke through.

'Do you think you're going to like it around here?'

'Oh yes, though it's a bit sad at first.'

'You'll settle in once you have children, you'll have put down roots here then.'

Geini had brought the kettle by this time. 'Make some tea for us, there's a good girl.'

'Do you know,' she said to Jane, 'I've got so that I don't really want to eat because it's too much trouble to prepare it.'

'And I tell you what,' she said to Geini once more, 'go and look for eggs in the hens' nests. People from Lleyn like eggs; we used to have two eggs wherever we went to tea.'

Jane laughed, beginning to feel at home.

'It was from Lleyn that I came here first, you see. But I don't remember much about living there now. I was only four years old when I came here, but I did go back once when I was a young girl at the end of one job because of a mix-up with beginning in my new place. I was a servant in a biggish farm down at the bottom end of this parish, and the work was too heavy for me. I gave in my notice before I had another place to go to, and there was no room for me to sleep at home, so I went to my Grandma in Lleyn. I walked there every step of the way. 'But,' said the old

19

woman, glancing around surreptitiously and placing her hand on Jane's knee as she spoke, 'How are things between you and Sioned? Has she been to see you yet?'

'Yes, last Monday morning.'

'Was she nice to you?'

'Well, no; I'm afraid I was a bit rude to her.'

'You can't be too rude with Sioned, in my opinion.'

And leaning close to Jane until her head was almost in the chimney, she whispered,

'Sioned is an old bitch, though I'm sorry to have to say such a thing about my own daughter-in-law. William suffered a lot because of her, and she didn't shed a tear when he died – the stupid creature. It all came to a strange end.'

'He was killed, wasn't he?'

'Yes, just as the hooter was going for the end of the shift one evening. He was gathering his things together and starting his way up the ladder when a big fall came down on him. But Sioned didn't grieve for him. Ifan was a son to her and a father to those children, and most of them quite big enough to look after themselves. The more you do in this world, the more they let you do. Don't you be too soft at the start, my girl. You stick to your guns if Sioned tries to get you under her thumb.'

At this Geini came back in.

'Your old hens are no good for laying, Grandma.'

'How many did you get?'

'Four.'

'Oh well, that'll do. Put two each for you two on the fire, and I'll have one – there's another in the bowl on the dresser.'

'Yes, I was just saying,' said the old woman, 'that I'd gone to stay with my grandma in Mynydd y Rhiw. I never came across kinder people in my life. Grandma and I were invited to tea every day just about, and that's what we were given – eggs – never one, always two – or boiled salted herring with jacket potatoes, or a fried salted plaice.'

'And in those days there weren't any houses that you could really call houses there, any more than there were around here. There weren't any proper roads then. And a house was just four walls and a thatched roof in those days, a peat fire on the floor, and two box beds back to back with their ends pointing towards the kitchen. When there was a dead body in the house you had to sleep in the same room as the coffin. Dear me, things have changed. Everyone's got two big rooms now.'

The three women enjoyed their tea eaten at the round white table without a cloth.

On the way back over the mountain, Jane couldn't help smiling when she thought of the old woman waiting to see the back of Geini before she disparaged her daughter-in-law. It was obvious that people were the same in every generation. And yet, she felt closer to the old woman than to anyone else in her new family except for Geini, despite her disloyalty, or perhaps because of it – or perhaps simply because she originally came from Lleyn. It was strange how such little things could draw people together in the bonds of affection.

4

Elin, the older child, sat upright as a poker on the table, having been told firmly that she was not to move. At that moment she had no desire to move, since it was so hot, and the strap of her bonnet was itching under her chin. On the rocking chair sat her mother struggling to pull a dress over the head of the younger baby – Sioned, who was flatly refusing to put her arm into the sleeve, insisting on putting her fist to her mouth and dribbling all over the clean dress before her mother had a chance to get a bib. She was so lively that the mother could scarcely hold her on her lap long enough to change her nappy and button her apron.

Then the mother hurried out carrying the two infants to the old-fashioned pram that stood in the yard in front of the house, and put them both to sit side by side on the long seat. Then she strapped them in tightly to prevent the younger one from falling out, placing the oilcloth over their feet. Sometimes their mother thought that taking the children out for a walk like this wasn't worth the bother of rushing to finish her work in the house during the morning. She made dough the night before sometimes and left it to rise overnight, lighting the fire at five in the morning so as to get the baking done. She would be exhausted before starting out. But it was a chance to keep the children quiet and a chance for a chat with someone on the road when she took them out like this.

With two cows and a calf, two pigs, and two babies – one two and a quarter and the other six months old – she had no time to visit anyone even if she'd wanted to. She couldn't go to anyone's house for 'elevenses' as other women did who had no smallholding to look after. As someone who didn't know the history of the neighbourhood, that was just as well, since she wouldn't be able to understand the references in the small talk that went on. She enjoyed taking the children out like this, enjoyed dressing them in their red twill dresses, their white petticoats with embroidered hems, and their starched bonnets. She felt that life was good. She had not yet experienced want. The money for the pigs paid the rates and the interest on the loan they had taken out to buy the small farm, and sometimes they were able to pay off some of the debt from the salary. One day they would pay it off, and the farm would belong to them.

It was of such things that Jane Gruffydd thought as she pushed the pram towards the mountain. Sometimes she felt a pang of regret that the two children in front of her weren't boys – they would have brought more money to the household than girls. But really Elin and Sioned were pretty little things. To her, from behind, they looked comical, the peaks of their bonnets sticking up straight and Sioned's yellow ringlets peeping through the holes in the needlework. Sioned leaned forward against the harness in her eagerness to grab at anything, while Elin sat up straight, giving Sioned an occasional slap.

They reached the cart-track that led to the mountain, the same mountain they had climbed over in going to Ifan's Grandma's house. The road was narrow and hard underfoot. Round about them was the heather and gorse, wet moss and peat bog. The gorse bushes were small and springy, their flowers of the palest yellow like primroses, contrasting with the colour of the stubby heather and the dark earth all around. Little streams ran from the mountain down onto the road, and the glistening water flowed on then, along the gravel at the side. Sometimes the stream would flow into a pool and would remain still there. The sheep tracks criss-crossed the mountain all over, and the sheep and long-tailed mountain ponies grazed everywhere. Everything connected to the mountain was small – the gorse, the moss, the sheep, the ponies. The silence was broken by the cry of the lapwing flying on her way and landing suddenly on the mountainside and then running to her nest in a little hollow – the indentation of a horseshoe, perhaps.

Jane liked to have a rest, taking the children out of the pram and putting them to sit on a shawl on the mountainside, while she herself sat down to dream. It was her own life that she dreamed about. She had no time except on a lazy May afternoon like this to wonder whether she was happy or not. She didn't put the question to herself very often. She had been very happy during the season of courtship; but she had enough common sense to realize that life could not carry on at that climactic pitch. Ifan was everything she wanted him to be, but he looked much more weary now than when she had first seen him those times he'd visited Lleyn with Guto the drover. In her own mind she was quite sure that working in the quarry and keeping a smallholding was simply too much work for him. But what could be done about it? She knew enough about the quarries, from hearsay, to know that a quarryman's pay was highly unreliable, and besides it was a good thing always to be able to rely on having plenty of milk and butter. One thing bothered her a great deal, and that was the state of the house. The kitchen where they lived was the only cosy room in it. The bedrooms, especially the one at the back, were damp and completely unhealthy for anyone to sleep in them. The dampness ran down the walls, ruining the wallpaper, and when there was frost and ice, drops of water would fall from the wooden ceiling onto the bed. She would have liked to have a new extension built onto the old house, so that she would have a front kitchen and at least two bedrooms. There were plenty of stones on the land of Ffridd Felen to build such an extension, and to get rid of those stones would be an improvement to the land itself. But Ifan would have to lay charges to extract the stone, and that would mean even more work for him. So, what was the point of dreaming?

She gazed at the distant village lying in the stillness of the afternoon. Up on the left was the quarry and its tip which thrust its snout down the mountainside like a snake. From afar, the stones in the rubble tip looked black, and they glittered in the sunshine. This was the quarry where Ifan's father had been killed. Who, she wondered, had emptied the first waggon of waste at the base of that tip? He was certainly in his grave by now. And who would be the last to throw his load of rubble from the top? What was she, Jane Gruffydd, a young woman from Lleyn, good for in this place? But after all, it was no worse for her here than in Lleyn. She had to be somewhere. And what was the good of dreaming?

A lamb's sad bleat came from afar, and the honking of geese from a nearby farm. There was something forlorn in the entire scene, the quarry, the village, and the mountain all tied up in each other. But then the next minute Jane was happy again, she and her children, happier perhaps than she would be for a long time to come.

5

Ifan was very ill with pneumonia, and Jane felt that it was all her fault. She had not been able to stop herself mentioning to him her plan to build an extension to the house, and the idea infected him like a disease. He didn't rest until he had collected enough stones from his land to be able to build the new extension. Every evening and Saturday afternoon the echo of his hammer and chisel was heard all over the neighbourhood, and then the sudden bang of the explosion. And now before the house was ready he was struck down by illness, brought on by the hard work. After a few years of undisturbed and uneventful existence, Jane found herself standing in the eye of a storm where every minute was as long as every year of her life since her marriage. She felt that she had not really been alive before. She regretted ever mentioning the dampness of the bedrooms to her husband. How on earth was she going to be able to pay the extra interest on the money that had been borrowed to build the extension if Ifan were to die? That was the thought that pained her at first. This pain insisted on thrusting itself into her heart, even though her conscience told her that only one thing should be on her mind, namely the pain of fearing her husband's death. As the days went on, the first pain receded in the face of the second.

During the nine days that Ifan lay between life and death Jane saw more of her in-laws than ever before, some of them for the first time. They trailed in one after the other, shook their heads at his bedside, but few offered to stay awake and on their feet through the night. Geini and Betsan, the oldest sister, were very good in this regard, though, while William lived too far away to be able to stay overnight. As for the rest, they arrived and spread their wings around the bed, as if they wanted to keep Jane from getting too close to the invalid. Their presence was like a siege on a town, and Jane was glad to see the back of them. Sioned Gruffydd luxuriated in her grief, and swept around like a ship in full sail. If someone happened to bump into her outside the door as she was leaving, Jane would overhear her say, 'I'm his mother, you know,' in a doleful voice.

Jane and Geini, or Jane and Betsan, would stay on their feet, and Bob Ifans, from Twnt i'r Mynydd, and other neighbours would be there. Every two hours they would re-apply the flax-seed poultice. One night, when Ifan was very ill, the sweat pouring from his burning body, his breath short, and having just had a bout of coughing, the door and window wide open and Geini fanning him, his brother Edward came to see him. Jane hadn't seen this brother before, but his demeanour in the sickroom was as if he had come into his own house.

'Why don't you move that table from in front of the window so that he can get some more air?' he said.

'You could have done that, if you'd come earlier,' said Geini.

28

Seeing him prepare to move the table, Jane said, 'No, better leave the table where it is for now; the noise will be too much for him.'

Edward looked at the ceiling, which was very close to the top of his head, as if he would have liked to start moving that.

'If you're looking for something to do, why not sit down in this chair?' said Jane, who had been feeling for some time that members of her husband's family were overrunning the house. If Ifan was going to die, she wanted to be there alone with him. She didn't even want Geini's company. She felt her love for her husband overflowing from her, and yet she had no opportunity to say anything of what she was feeling in the midst of these family witnesses.

When she went to the kitchen, Edward whispered to Geini, 'Has he made his will?'

'Hush!' she said, so loudly that the invalid turned his head and groaned, licking his dry lips.

'Jane,' she said, 'bring water.'

And Jane rushed from the kitchen to give him a drink.

The following night he was worse, and his mother was sent for. But in the middle of the night, at about two in the morning, he started to become calmer. Sioned Gruffydd sat by the fire, asleep, while Bob Ifans and Betsan sat by the bedside. Jane walked quietly between the bedroom and the kitchen hearth. Finally she sat down by the fire. The kettle sang faintly on the hob. From the back bedroom came the snoring of one of the children. The invalid moaned from time to time. The clock ticked. An ember fell from the grate in the bedroom. The night air was heavy, and Jane fell asleep despite her anxiety. Sleep was stronger than her love.

She was awoken by the sound of Ifan's voice calling

her name. 'Jane,' he said, 'where are the children?'

And that was the first sign that he was on the mend.

For Jane, the months that followed were happy ones, though she still carried a burden of anxiety. She was like a man who had been saved from a shipwreck. Possessions were not important – the main thing was to be alive. To her, the whole financial mess with the building of the extension was nothing, after her husband began to get better. She had to do what she could to keep from him as long as possible that they were running up a debt in the shop.

There was nothing else to be done. She got only ten shillings a week from the Friendly Society. Strangely enough, she had been more worried about money and such things before Ifan fell ill. She felt that they had shouldered too much of a burden, and feared that the quarryman's wages would go down. Her husband would not be able to work for weeks, the Friendly Society money would dwindle, and even after that he wouldn't be able to work hard. Yet now that the burden upon her was so great she felt able to throw it off completely, and she refused even to think about it. It was enough for her that Ifan was alive. Nothing else mattered.

Her mother came to visit Ifan. She did not enquire about how they were making ends meet, and Jane told her nothing. But her mother gave her a sovereign before she left. She was prompted to this generosity not because of seeing her son-in-law looking grey and thin, but from pity at seeing her daughter living in such a poor neighbourhood. It's true that it was the beginning of winter, but the mistress of Sarn Goch could not imagine anything growing in that grey neighbourhood even at the height of summer.

6

Within a few months of Ifan's return to work, their third child was born and was named William; two years after that, another son was born and named Owen, and their parents had a far-off glimpse of the day when the two would be a help to them, after they started work in the quarry. William looked as if he was going to be a strong boy, but Owen was a bit of a weakling, though a weakling who was a very fast learner.

One night in January 1893 there was a children's evening in the chapel and all four of the children were there. It was to the chapel they went most often. They attended all the weekday services there, and their mother tended to go more often to the chapel than the church now, when she was able to go at all. Tonight was a bright moonlit night, with everything frozen solid underfoot. Before going to chapel all the children had been skating on the streams that flowed straight from the fields into the gully where the river ran through the village, if you could call a water-course about a foot wide a river. In weather like this the children would dash home from School as fast as their legs would carry them, though they were tempted to start skating on the way up. But it was better to hurry home, have their tea, and then go out to skate properly. On these short winter days they didn't actually have tea but broth when they arrived home, since it was so close to time for the quarry-supper, which was usually lobscouse in winter. The boys ate standing up without taking their coats off so as to be able to rush out again quickly. They all had to help afterwards, though, the girls doing the washing up and the boys fetching heather and coal to start the fire in the morning. Those were their regular tasks after coming home from School.

'Now then,' said their mother, emphasizing the *now*, 'if you're not going to be coming home before the meeting, you have to have a wash now. Owen, take your neckcloth off so that you can wash properly.' Owen grimaced. He thought he would be able to go and skate as soon as he'd finished his chores. But he was ready in no time, his face scrubbed bright red, and a wet, wayward tuft of hair sticking straight out beneath the peak of his cap. He put the long scarf back around his throat, till there was nothing to be seen of him except his nose and eyes. The boys wore short, double-breasted coats, called monkey-jackets. The girls wore similar short coats over their aprons. They had white furs around their throats, like sheep's tails, tied with ribbons under their chins, and caps something like those of their brothers on their heads.

There was a full moon, almost as yellow as it is in September. The wind blew like a knife through the children's clothing, and their eyes watered and mucus ran from their noses, dripping in one big drop to the ground. They sang as they went along, or rather they recited rhythmically:

32

Moon shining,
Children playing,
Bandits coming,
Socks a-knitting,
'A-men,' said the stake,
From John's shop we'll steal a cake.
John, John, will you have some gin?
I will, I will, if it's for nothing.

All the children going to the chapel meeting were
above the gully skating, each one longing for his or her turn
to go on the slide. They didn't wait for one to finish sliding
while they all stood and watched. Instead, they went
whizzing off one after another, and the trick was to skid off
the slide before it reached the gully. The boys did this by
bending their bodies from one side to the other, keeping
their arms raised in the air to steer themselves. But the girls
tended to keep their hands in their pockets, and so they
found it harder to escape from the slide before its end.
Owen did the same as the girls, but his trick failed and so
he had to leap right across the gully from one side to the
other. He landed so heavily on his feet that the pain coursed
through his body like thousands of pins, and he felt as if
he'd knocked his head and not his feet. Nobody had time
to see whether he was hurt. He ran up the gully to where
he could cross the river and then went back to the slide.

'You daft fool,' said some boy to him, 'why didn't you
lift your arms up?'

'I *wanted* to jump across,' he replied.

'You watch out that you don't land in the middle of
the river,' said someone else.

The 'daft fool' got right under Owen's skin. He couldn't get the words or the tone of voice they were said in out of his head. Nor could he take his turn on the slide again. The truth was that he had not been trying to leap across the gully, but he had been more or less hurled across by the crowd of big boys coming behind him, and he so little. He felt almost as if he were being shoved across and the best thing to do was to jump clear, and he thought he had been quite skilful in managing to get over the gully. The other boys and girls kept on sliding one after the other, tirelessly and continuously, and with their arms up in the air like that and their bodies at a slant they looked like swallows on the wing.

Before long, Elin noticed that Owen wasn't skating any more.

'Why have you stopped?' she said.

But Owen didn't say a word.

'Now then, go on, don't be daft'.

'I'm *not* daft,' he said hotly, 'and I'll show you that I'm not too.'

He took a run up, and off he went on the slide, and since the others had been listening to him and Elin, and thinking that something was up, they stopped sliding themselves, so that Owen had it all to himself. He slid along it as light as a feather, and managed to turn off it before he reached the end, at which he gained tumultuous applause.

In the children's meeting later everyone was surprised to see Owen go forward to try his hand at almost everything. The chapel felt cold after the skating. They arrived there in a boisterous mob, their hands and faces red. Only in the lower part of the chapel were the lamps lit, and the children's lengthy shadows were thrown onto the unlit sections, while the chairman, who was sitting in the deacons' Big Seat, had only half his face illuminated.

'You're not to come,' said Sioned, when she saw Owen getting ready to go into the lobby when the competition for Welsh translation of English words came up.

'Yes I am coming,' said Owen, putting his cap in his pocket.

'What do you know about translating English to Welsh?' said William. 'You're too small.'

'You'll soon see,' said Owen.

The lobby was dark, and the bigger children were enjoying themselves by pinching and sticking pins in each other, and when a man came to look at what they were up to they stuck a pin in him as well. He reached out his arm and gave the child nearest to him a clout. Owen crouched down among the others, his heart racing with fear and happiness. All sorts of feelings were coursing through his body; from time to time he found himself swallowing hard and at other times he felt light-headed as if he were going to faint. Before long, the chapel door opened, and the light fell on the faces of those children closest to the doorway.

'Next,' said a voice, and Owen slipped inside.

'Well, the little devil,' said some boy behind him, 'That was my turn.'

Owen went to the Big Seat, feeling that he would be unable to utter a word. But when the man said 'Give the correct Welsh word for "to use",' Owen answered like a bullet,

'Defnyddio.'

'Cabbage'... 'Bresych.'

'Trousers'... 'Llodrau.'

'Station' ... 'Gorsaf.'

And so it went on right to the end of the test. Owen was right every time. The same happened in the competition to read a passage without punctuation aloud, to give directions to a stranger, and recitation. Owen won every single competition, and he went home with a shilling and sixpence in pennies in his pocket.

He galloped home, with the horseshoe from the sole of his clog in his pocket ever since the skating earlier. But his face fell when he saw that there was a stranger in the house. He should have remembered that Ann Ifans Twnt i'r Mynydd would often visit when there was a children's meeting in the evening. She brought her children to the chapel, and then she would wait in Ffridd Felen with Jane and Ifan Gruffydd until they came home. The children from Twnt i'r Mynydd would then have supper with the Ffridd Felen children. Owen had forgotten about this and his face fell, because he wanted to have the house to himself to tell his mother and father the story of his triumph.

'Where are the other children?' was his mother's first question.

'They're on their way,' he replied.

If his mother had asked 'Well, what did you get in the meeting?' he would have had a good opportunity to pour out his news. But it was clear to Owen that his mother felt that he would be unable to win anything. Since he was the fourth child, he had learned to read under the noses of the older children and they had not really noticed how quick he had been, because they had been quite sharp themselves.

The troop of children arrived at the house.

'Crikey, Owen has outdone us all tonight.'

The three adults turned their heads to look at him in astonishment.

'He won every single competition except the singing.'

'How much money did you get?' asked John Twnt i'r

Mynydd.

'One and six,' said Owen shyly, 'and the rim of my clog has come off!'

Everyone laughed except his father.

'Damn it all,' he said, for he disliked nothing more than having to go and look for his nail box when he was about ready to go to bed. Owen felt that the lustre was starting to pall on his shilling-and-sixpence while he listened to his father grumbling as he nailed the horseshoe back onto the clog. But everything was alright again afterwards as the children ate their supper of tea, bread and butter and cheese together, for his father was smiling again like everyone else by that time.

Ann Ifans was a genial, funny woman and while the children were at chapel she had entertained Jane and Ifan with her funny stories. Her biggest complaint against life was that she was cut off from civilization. She was literally cut off from the village whenever it snowed. The tops of the hedges would be the path to her house then. And her greatest consolation was company. A moonlit night was as good as a gift for her. Nothing much else bothered her at all. She turned a prophetic eye on the children as they ate their supper.

'Who knows what these children will turn out to be one day. Maybe Owen here will end up as a banker.'

All the children laughed, thinking of the money Owen had in his pocket.

'He's starting the banking business right now,' said John.

'His mother has plenty of room to keep that money,' said his father.

Owen frowned.

'Don't take any notice, Owen,' said Ann Ifans, 'perhaps you'll be a millionaire one day, riding in a closed carriage, and your mother wearing a veil.'

After the Twnt i'r Mynydd family had left, his mother asked Owen,

'Aren't you going to give that money to your mother?'

'No I'm not,' said Owen straight away. His mother looked at his father, and his father looked at Owen, in a way which suggested that Owen had sinned against the Almighty.

'Give the money to your mother now, none of your nonsense,' said his father. 'She needs it to buy food for you.'

'I need it to buy an exercise book and a rubber and pencil,' said Owen.

'It's more important for you to have food than things like that,' said his mother.

Owen threw the money on the table in a temper, and got a clip around the ear for it from his mother. He burst out crying loudly, and was still crying when he went to bed. He wept for ages after laying his head on the pillow.

'Stop your howling,' said William, 'I want to go to sleep.'

He carried on weeping silently after that.

'There now,' whispered a voice from above after a little while, 'never you mind, I'll buy you an exercise book.'

It was Elin, who had come over in her nightdress when she heard him crying. She wasn't certain if she would be able to get a penny from somewhere, but she thought it was worth promising it to him. The promise pacified Owen, since it meant that at least there was someone in the house who understood what he wanted.

This was the first time he became aware of the struggle against poverty that went on in his home. He hadn't the slightest idea where his food and clothes came from. They just came regularly day after day, and he had never thought about how they did so. He failed to see that his prize money would buy much food for anyone. His sadness was immeasurable. He kept sighing. This was the first time he had ever been really sad, and it was an unexpected sadness at that. His feelings had been hurt on the slide, but his victory in the children's meeting had been enough to make him forget about that, and he had run home thinking about the welcome he would have, and about how proud his father and mother would be that he wanted to buy a copy book rather than sweets. He hadn't foreseen any of this. He had even felt happy as he ate his supper, for he was fond of Ann Ifans and her children. She had bright blue eyes and always had a funny story to tell. Her children weren't very clever, but they weren't jealous and even admired those who were. He had enjoyed the way Ann Ifans had looked at him over supper.

But now his whole happiness was in pieces. His father was in a bad mood because he'd had to mend his clog, and his mother had given him a clout because he'd thrown the money on the table. And here he was, having beaten children older than him in every single competition! No one had said a word about that, except what was expressed in Ann Ifans's look.

He had noticed several times recently that his mother looked sad. She sometimes looked sad when the pigs were taken away. Owen didn't understand that since she got money for them (this money was always kept in a separate box). But his mother said that the price of pigs went down every time she had a litter ready to sell. 'If I'd sold them a fortnight ago, I would have had fourpence and a farthing

39

instead of fourpence and a half-farthing.'* And then there was that day when the calf died; his mother had cried. Then it had been horribly sad when they'd had to sell a young heifer to the butcher because she had only three teats. Owen didn't understand why one teat fewer made any difference to a cow as long as she had an udder. And then they got money for that cow but Owen heard them talk about having to spend money again straight away to get another cow.

He remembered asking his mother one day,

'Mam, how would it be if there was nothing at all?'

'How do you mean?'

'What if there was *nothing*, nothing there (pointing at the sky), and nothing anywhere else, and we didn't exist either?'

'It would be lovely, my boy,' was her only answer.

He came to connect his mother's sad look with every grown-up he knew. But no, Ann Ifans was different.

Owen failed to understand things, and tonight in his bed he began to think that that answer of his mother's had something to do with the fact that she didn't have enough money to get food. But things were still very unclear to him, and he finally went to sleep.

In her bedroom his mother was worried that she had been so nasty to Owen. She should have been glad that he had won so many prizes and had shown that he had plenty of brains. She should have won him over by being nice to him instead of losing her temper. That wouldn't have been difficult since Owen was the only one of the older children whose world turned around his mother. But struggling and struggling to make ends meet had made her short-tempered. Meanwhile Ifan slept the deep sleep of the quarryman.

The next morning Owen had more or less got over it,

40

but he still had the occasional pang when he remembered what had happened. As he went through the gate to School, his mother called him back and gave him threepence.

'Here,' she said, 'buy a copybook and those things with that. You'll get better ones some day.'

Owen was too shy to express how glad he was, but he said, with his eyes shining,

'I'll come with you to church on Sunday.'

7

In the year 1899 Owen won a scholarship to the County School. Since there were only six scholarships to be had at that time, and since he was competing against the children from the town and had to write in English, this was quite a feat. Owen had set his heart on going to the County School, but felt after sitting the exam that he had no hope of getting in. He was one of those children who had no confidence in himself in an examination, or as the neighbours said, 'there was no get up and go in him.' For months beforehand he had been worried, not about the exam itself, but about the things surrounding it: where was the entrance to the School, where would he sit, how would he ask for more paper. He didn't sleep much the night before. He admired the other boys' nonchalant attitude as they walked to town on that morning. But as he found out dozens of times later in his life, the whole thing wasn't half as bad as he had expected.

One Saturday afternoon towards the end of July, a rumour came through the neighbourhood that he had won a scholarship. The news was brought by the people who travelled on the brake from town. The brake went to town and back three times a week. On Saturdays it went in four times and when it came back at midday Morgan Huws, the owner of the brake, told someone that he had spoken to somebody who had heard from the clerk to the governors of the County School that Owen was at the top of the list of boys who had gained a place. Owen heard the news while he was in the village and he ran home like lightning, collapsing in a heap on a chair when he got there. Achieving his goal on the first attempt was all too much for him.

There was no one in the house except his mother, and when she heard the news she was astonished, since for so many years, she felt, things had gone against her rather than in her favour. For a minute she was unable to take in what had happened. When she began to come to herself, so many things flashed through her mind that she couldn't say a word. One minute she felt herself swelling up with pride that it was her child who had won the scholarship; the next minute her heart sank as she thought that Ifan might be disappointed. Wages at the quarry were exceptionally low, and the head of every household these days was glad to have his son go to the quarry with him; they then got a chance to increase their own wages by staying behind to work with their boys. She also had the notion that it would cost considerably more to send Owen to the County School than to the Primary School. Owen's voice broke through her thoughts.

'Aren't you pleased, mam?'

'Yes, it's just that I'm thinking it over.'

'Thinking what over?'

'What will your father say?'

'Why, what will he have to say?'

43

'He could make you go to the quarry.'

This possibility had not even dawned on Owen.

'Why?'

'Perhaps we won't have the means to send you to the Middle School.'

'But you don't need money because I've won the scholarship.'

'No, but you see, perhaps your father will want you to go to the quarry so as to earn some money.'

Owen fell silent. He had not thought that anyone would object. And once more, he became downhearted as he saw himself facing what he would later call a financial problem.

His father came home, and didn't look much happier than his mother had been at the news. He was doubtful whether the news was true. His mother roused herself.

'Ifan,' she said, 'you go to town and find out if it's true. It's a while since you were there. You go too, Owen.'

'No, I don't want to go,' said Owen.

'You don't want to go to town!'

'No, I'd rather stay at home. Maybe the news isn't true.'

At any other time Owen would have jumped at the chance. But going to town to enquire about something that might turn out to be a disappointment was very different from going to town on Ascension Day, when his father's Club had a procession, to see the band marching, and being able to spend more than a halfpenny, the most he was allowed to spend on his way to School. He would have to wait many hours before he found out the truth.

He went into the field and lay down on the earth with his face towards the sun, and turned things over in his mind. He remembered that evening of the children's

44

meeting at the chapel, when he got a clout for throwing his prizemoney on the table; that evening when he had first realized that food and clothing were not to be had for nothing. He remembered Ann Ifans's happy face that night, and the difference between that face and his mother's. He was disappointed that no one seemed particularly glad that he seemed to have won the scholarship.

Somehow or other, no one ever seemed to be glad at all in his home. Will was too tired after coming home from the quarry. He dragged his feet in their heavy hobnailed boots towards the house, and his corduroy trousers hung loosely upon him. Perhaps it would be best for him to go to the quarry like Will. It would be less painful in the long run. Will was quite clever, but he would have to work in the quarry forever, it seemed, and it wasn't fair for him, Owen, to have the opportunity that his brother didn't have. No; he felt that he had to be allowed to go to the Middle School.

What with the heat and the worry, the sweat was pouring off his body. He turned his face away from the sun. The earth beneath him was hot, as if it too were in a sweat. With one eye Owen could see the new growth springing up green and fresh amongst the hard, dry stubble. The cat came up to him and rubbed her soft fur against his face. The sunshine fell on her fur, and penetrated through to the skin which showed up pink, as you see your own flesh when you hold it up between you and the light. The cat interfered with his breathing as she rubbed herself on his skin, and he gave her a shove to get her to go away. She turned around and around as if she didn't know what to do, and the hard stubble made her pick her paws up affectedly as she walked. She came up to him again and put her head lovingly next to his face.

45

He sat up. The land lying round about him was beautiful. The sea was blue, with the island of Anglesey lying far off in the distance bathed in a soft heat haze. There was the County School, a red smudge just visible on the horizon. Next to it was Llanfeuno* cemetery, whose marble gravestones were glittering like hundreds of diamonds in the sunshine. The fields around him were quiet and dreamy, and at that moment Owen loved them. Deep in his unconscious he probably loved them all the time. He realized that before long he wouldn't be able to spend so much time on the land of Ffridd Felen. Over there in the bottom corner of the field was the wild raspberry bush. He remembered the thrill of delight that came over him when he first found the raspberries and realized that they were the same things that grew in gardens except they were smaller. On his left was the bilberry bush that stood out greenly against the rest of the hedge, in the middle of the yellow of the gorse and the purple heather. The bilberries were a big draw every June and July.

Now he remembered – his mother would have a bilberry tart for tea. But the house was hot, since his mother had been baking all morning and roasting the meat for Sunday dinner. It had been like a furnace already at dinner time. Despite this, he got to his feet and went towards the house. His father wouldn't be home for ages. The table was already laid for tea, and William was eating and in his clean clothes. He looked less wornout in his best clothes with his starched collar, but he looked so hot that it made Owen throw off his own rubber collar. William was having his tea early so as to be able to go out with the lads.

'You can have your tea now in a minute, with me,' Owen's mother said to him.

The kitchen was cooler by this time, and there were just a few flames coming from the cowdung in the fireplace, the kettle simmering gently above.

'Where are Twm and Bet?' asked Owen.

'The two of them have gone up the mountain with the Manod* children to gather whinberries,' said his mother.

'Are you tired, my boy?' she asked then, seeing the overheated look on Owen's face.

'I've been lying in the sun. When will dad be home?'

'Not for hours yet, so don't worry about it.'

And indeed, in that moment, he was able to stop thinking about the scholarship. He always felt happy when his mother was friendly like this. The tea and the berry tart were good. The house was comfortable too, with its oak furniture gleaming, the bread placed beside it on the floor to cool down, and a hint of the aroma of all the baking floating around in the kitchen. His mother was wearing a light cotton frock with a lilac flower pattern. Owen thought his mother looked good in this frock. Her hair looked darker somehow, and her skin clearer. Why wasn't his home always like this? What was the point of worrying about things? By this time he couldn't have cared less whether he had got the scholarship or not. He felt well disposed to everybody, and to his mother in particular.

Twm and Bet came home before long, carrying a few whinberries in the bottom of a jug. Twm was seven, and Bet four. There had been quite a big gap for Jane Gruffydd between Owen and Twm. And just as they sat down to eat, aunt Geini dashed into the house.

'Is it true?' were her first words.

'I don't know,' said Jane, 'Ifan has gone into town to find out.'

47

'Oh, I hope it is true,' said Geini, almost too excited to sit down.

'Even if it is true, I'm not sure we'll be able to afford to send him to the School.'

'What? Of course you can. It would be a sin to stop the boy going.'

'He'd be able to earn a bit of money in the quarry if his father helped him, and you know what a burden it is for us to pay for this new house.'

'But then, one day he'll be able to bring in more money for you after he finishes his education.'

'That's questionable,' said Jane Gruffydd.

'Yes, of course I will,' said Owen.

The two women found something especially endearing in Owen when he said this. As for him, he felt like throwing his arms around his aunt Geini for sticking up for him.

'I'm expecting Sioned home any minute,' said his mother.

'Oh, sorry to interrupt but I just saw her going over to see mother, and she told me to tell you not to expect her. She's going to have her supper with mam.'

Jane frowned, obviously displeased. Sioned was almost seventeen years old and attending a sewing School in Pont Garrog. She had started work as a maidservant after leaving School, like her sister Elin, but she failed to get on with two mistresses, and then said that she wanted to be a seamstress instead. In this she was supported by her grandmother. Sioned Gruffydd had started taking an interest in her granddaughter at the time when Ifan was ill, and by now Sioned lived in her grandmother's house whenever she had a day off.

At sixteen, she was a tall, pretty, fair-complexioned girl.

Her hair was a light amber colour, with a broad wave in it. Her eyes were hazel and turned up slightly at the outer corners. Her skin was like cream, with hardly a hint of a blush. Ever since she began her apprenticeship she had become completely obsessed with clothes, and when she was unable to persuade her mother to give her money to buy dress material she would sneak over to her grandmother and wheedle the money out of her. Recently she had begun to go to her grandmother's house directly from work on a Saturday afternoon, and the little time she did spend at home it was as if she were locked away in her own little world, and had nothing to say to anyone. She tended to snap whenever anyone tried to start a conversation with her.

One morning when she turned up her nose at her breakfast of tea and bread and butter, her mother got the opportunity of doing what she had been meaning to do for months on end, namely, to ask her, seriously, what was the matter with her.

Sioned lost her temper, and showed pretty clearly that she now felt herself to be too high and mighty for Ffridd Felen.

'A hole like this,' she said, 'in the back of beyond, stuck in a time warp, and having to eat the same old thing day after day.'

Jane Gruffydd was so astonished that she could barely utter a word. To think that her own child should say such things! And in her heart of hearts, Jane Gruffydd was rather proud of her cooking.

Without raising her voice, she said,

'Maybe you'll be glad of this food one day. You certainly won't get anything better in your grandmother's house.'

The row had cleared the air for a while. But recently Sioned had started to go to her grandmother's house more often once again. No wonder, then, that her mother looked disgruntled when she heard Geini say that Sioned had gone straight from work to her grandmother's house.

Ifan came home by the eight o'clock brake, and no one needed to ask whether Owen had got the scholarship. His father was astonishingly happy, his eyes glittering with joy. It seemed to Owen that he'd gone cross-eyed. There was a red line on his forehead where his hat had been, and the sweat ran down from this line to pause, dripping, on his temples. There were different smells in the house now too, smells that Owen could not identify.

In the brake on the way down Ifan had worked out how to discover whether the news was true or not. Elin worked as a servant in a lawyer's house in town, and he felt sure that he would be able to get the truth from her.

And so it was that he made the discovery. Elin was the first in the family to show real enthusiasm for the thing, and she succeeded in persuading her father that it was nonsense to send Owen to the quarry instead of to the School.

Later, in town he met one of his partners in the quarry, Guto Cerrig Duon, and the two went to celebrate the news in the Fox and Horses by treating each other to a pint of beer. As he came out of the pub, Ifan ran straight into Dolly Rhyd Garreg and her daughter, Gwen. It was impossible to avoid her, and under the influence of the beer and the news he couldn't find it in himself to be less than nice to her.

Dolly was wearing a short black satin jacket which reached just below her waist. She had a black toque on her head with little black shiny things like a herring's scales scattered upon it. There was a very prosperous air about her and her daughter, Gwen, who was wearing a good leghorn hat and a red dress of French merino.

'I've just heard the good news about your little boy,' said Dolly.

(She had actually found out that morning and that's what had brought her into town.)

'Yes,' said Ifan in a jubilant, loud voice 'he came top of the list.'

'Yes, the top among the boys, wasn't it?' said Dolly in a velvety voice. 'My daughter came fifth.'

'Yes, the fifth of the girls, wasn't it, and only three boys and three girls can get it for free,' said Ifan in the same tone of voice as her.

'We'll be paying for Gwen to go, it's often the case that the ones like Gwen end up doing better than the ones who were top in the scholarship exam.'

'I'm sure you're right. Good day now,' said Ifan, and off he went towards the brake.

Ifan told this story later with his eyes flashing in mockery.

'Well,' said his wife, 'Owen shall go to the Middle School, if it's only to spite Dolly Rhyd Garreg.'

'No,' said Ifan, 'Owen shall go to the School so that he can be educated. He can go through this world then, and noone can steal that education from him.'

Ifan had learned his lesson from Elin, and his attitude was so different from what it had been when he left to go to town that everyone laughed.

'I never heard you talk such sense,' said Geini.

Ifan had brought brawn home for supper, and Geini was persuaded to stay to eat with them.

They were all content until Ifan asked 'Where's Sioned?'

She's back home with Mam,' said Geini. 'There's no need for you to keep any of this brawn for her, she will have had her supper.'

Jane hid her face so that no one could see her expression.

Sioned came home at about ten, her face red and her eyes sparkling. She was bathed in sweat after running home, but the light in her eyes was unmistakably the light of first love. She had left her grandmother's house at six and had met Dic Edwards, a shop worker from town, in Ceunant Forest. She had gone without supper in order to meet him, and in her bed she tossed and turned, reliving the evening until the small hours.

In her own bed, the mother lay awake for a long time trying to interpret Sioned's joyful look.

In his bed, Owen thought about his father and his strangely cross-eyed look, and laughed to himself. Then he smiled at the complete change in his parents' view of the scholarship in only a few hours. Indeed, grown-ups were strange beings, shifting and changing their minds from minute to minute. Then he remembered how pretty Sioned had looked when she came home.

William snored by his side. He and the younger children were the only ones who went straight to sleep.

8

Within six weeks Geini suddenly got married without letting anyone in the neighbourhood know. She was thirty-five years old by now, and no one thought that she would ever marry. She had been courting Eben Ffynnon Oer for many years but she couldn't marry him because she was, like her brother Ifan years before, loath to abandon her mother. Eben didn't stop asking, though each time it came to the point Geini wouldn't say yes, but something happened which made her change her mind all of a sudden.

Ever since the Saturday night when Sioned had started to go out with Dic Edwards, she had gone to her grandmother's house more often, and one night she asked her grandmother if she could stay overnight the next day. The latter agreed readily, and by the time she got home to Ffridd Felen Sioned had a pretty story to tell her mother, that she wanted to sew and remodel her grandmother's old clothes for her. Her mother absent-mindedly agreed, though she suspected that something was going on that she knew nothing about. She would have liked to go up to Y Fawnog to see what Sioned's scheme was really about, but that was the last thing she could do, since she knew that Sioned Gruffydd would simply side with her granddaughter, come what may. Jane's instincts told her that her mother-in-law was taking revenge on her by nurturing and siding with Sioned. She was expecting Geini to come down any day to talk it over with her, but Geini didn't come.

Sioned met her lover every night, and she turned up at her grandmother's house late with the excuse that she had been working late to help out because the seamstress was so busy. After the first few nights Geini started to have her doubts. It was not coming up to Easter or Whitsun, and it wasn't the start of the winter season. She felt like going down to the seamstress's house, but that would seem too much like snooping, and what if Sioned were telling the truth? But it put her into a bad temper. Even before this, relations between Geini and her mother could not have been called peaceable. They did not see eye to eye, they rowed, they sulked, and then made up with each other again. It would not be accurate to say that there was a 'reconciliation' because there was never agreement between them in the first place. But the two of them were evenly matched. It didn't matter which of the two got the last word, neither of them had anyone else on their side, so there was nothing to complain about on that score.

But now here was a cuckoo in the nest. Geini would have found it easier to bear if Sioned had made the slightest effort to be friendly towards her. But no, she barely spoke to her. She slept with her grandmother, an unhealthy practice in Geini's view. She was sure that Sioned had something to hide. She set off each morning wearing her black day dress and carrying a parcel under her arm, but then she returned to the house at night wearing her best dress and with a parcel under her arm. To Geini's eyes it was a sin to be wearing your best dress every day – a light purple dress, trimmed with folds of darker ribbon around the sleeve hems and across the front in a half-moon shape; the bodice and neckline of white satin covered in lace. Soon the dress would be too short for her. Did her mother know that she was wearing her best dress every day? She longed to go down to Ffridd Felen. But she might put her foot in it. She didn't want to create a fuss if she could help it. It could even cause bad feeling between Jane and Ifan.

However, on the fourth morning she couldn't stand it any more. She had been out feeding the pigs and the chickens after doing the milking, and she was coming to the house to have her breakfast. Sioned had just finished her breakfast of tea, bread and butter and an egg, and was looking at herself in the mirror before setting off. She saw her mother getting some money out of her purse in the drawer of the dresser. Sioned went out of the front door and her grandmother followed her, and Geini knew that money had changed hands. This made Geini angry. She also remembered the night before, when Sioned had sat in the armchair like a lady, her legs stretched out on the hearth. She banged about with the dishes, and made a terrific noise preparing her own breakfast.

'What are you making such a racket for?'
'I'd like to know what you were giving Sioned.'
'Is it anybody's business what I was giving her?'
'Yes, it's my business.'
'Since when?'
'Ever since I've been working and slaving away here. It comes to something when I work hard to make money, and you just give it away to a creature like that.'

'If you're not content, you know what you can do.'

'Yes, I do, and I know what you'll have to do as well.'

'Sioned will come and live here with me.'

Geini laughed loudly.

'I can just see that lady giving the calves their mash. Ha ha ha!'

That night Geini went to Eben and told him that she would marry him.

On her way back she called in at Ffridd Felen; she had decided to tell Sioned's parents everything about her. But she was spared that task. Everything was in chaos there, ever since Ifan had got home from the quarry.

Morris Ifan, Dolly Rhyd Garreg's husband, who was the Little Steward by this time, had called Ifan into the office in the quarry. Buckley the Steward wasn't there that day.

The deputy foreman was always called the Little Steward but Morris was in fact little in every sense. His abilities as a steward were so paltry that he was afraid that he might lose his job and so, typical for a man like that, he held the reins around the workers' necks all the more tightly. He was afraid of the workers because he was afraid of his own incompetence. But he worked in cahoots with the Steward and therefore into the hands of the owners. Ifan's life in the quarry had never been happy ever since the Little Steward had married Dolly. He did not victimize him openly but in his presence Ifan always felt as if a little cat were playing with him. The cat's paws were soft and velvety, but the claws could suddenly be unsheathed at any moment. And Ifan suspected that today he was going to see those claws.

'Sit down, Ifan Gruffydd,' said Morris Ifan.

Ifan did so, placing his dusty hard hat on his knee.

'What I've got to say to you has nothing to do with the quarry,' said the Little Steward, playing with his watch chain, 'but I feel that I have to speak to you about the conduct of your daughter, Sioned.'

'Sioned! What has Sioned done?'

'Well, I'm very sorry to have to tell you this, but I've seen her two or three times recently with some boy in Ceunant Forest.'

'Are you sure about that? – because she goes straight from work to her grandmother's house, to do some sewing for her, and she stays overnight there afterwards.'

The Steward smiled suggestively, like someone familiar with the tricks of young people when they're courting. Ifan saw that and blushed.

'Was she doing something wrong?' was his next question.

'Oh no, she wasn't, but I thought you wouldn't be pleased to learn that your daughter, and her still so young, was sitting in Ceunant Forest with a young man putting his arm around her waist.'

Ifan was about to answer him, when he remembered that he was a worker and the other man an official, and times were bad.

'Thank you for letting me know,' said Ifan politely, and turned on his heel.

The Steward felt disappointed after Ifan had left the office. He had expected him to answer back so that he would have a hold on him forever after.

This happened just before the hooter sounded, so Ifan didn't have to face any of his fellow-workers with the burden he now had on his mind. On his way home, his mouth talked to his fellows but his mind was talking to itself. Why hadn't he spoken his mind to that nosy little sneak? If he had been going for a walk in Ceunant Forest the first night he'd seen Sioned, Ifan was sure that he hadn't been going for a walk the next time and the time after that. And yet, it was for the best that he had been able to keep his mouth shut. Wages were low, and it was a favour to be allowed to work much with your son these days. The Steward could easily give him the sack, since he and the Little Steward were thick as thieves. But oh! Ifan was deeply ashamed. If his work partner had told him this he would have known that he was doing it from genuine concern, but he knew that it was the pleasure of taking Ifan down a peg or two that motivated the Little Steward.

Then he turned his thoughts to Sioned herself. What was to be done with her? He himself had not been much older when he started courting Dolly. He couldn't blame her for courting. Yet she was very young, and times were changing. In Ifan's youth young men would be earning enough to keep a wife before boys even left School these days. She went to her grandmother's house far too much as it was, without making it a haven to hide in and blind her parents to what she was up to.

He sighed as he hung his hat on the nail, and Jane knew immediately that something was wrong, from the sound of his sighing.

After they had eaten their quarry supper, Owen's mother said to him, 'Look, why don't you go over to Twnt i'r Mynydd? You haven't been there for ages.'

At any other time, Owen would have been happy to go, but today he knew from the tense atmosphere that he was being sent out of the way. Twm and Bet had not come back from their wanderings. They were hardly to be seen on these

58

long summer days. Of the children only Owen and William were there. Owen started out unwillingly, dragging his feet.

'Can I wear my best shoes? I'm fed up with these.'

'Yes you can,' said his mother, feeling suddenly sorry for him.

Once Owen had gone, Ifan told William and Jane what the Little Steward had said.

Since she had had her suspicions for some time, Jane was not particularly surprised. What made her angry was that the thing had gone on for so long because Sioned had been able to cover it up by staying in her grandmother's house. If Sioned had tried to fool them at home, she would have been found out long ago.

'It's our fault for allowing your mother to cover up for her for so long,' said Jane.

'Yes, you're right,' said Ifan impatiently, 'but it was Sioned who chose to go there.'

'Yes, like a calf after a sugar lump,' she said.

'She went there without the sugar this time,' said Ifan.

For a moment, Ifan was indignant with Jane for blaming his mother more than Sioned herself.

To him a thing such as this was a kind of mental irritation, interfering with his quiet life. It began to dawn on him that children were more trouble than they were worth. All he wanted was plenty of work and good stones in the quarry, to be able to work on the smallholding when he came home, and then a smoke and a newspaper before bed. But ever since the children started growing up there was some trouble over them all the time. As soon as they got old enough to cross the threshold there was no knowing from which direction the next problem would come along. What weighed heaviest on Ifan's mind was

59

how he was going to go to his mother's house to fetch Sioned. He was a man who was never worn out by the demands of work, and he was able to deal with all kinds of difficulties in the quarry, but once something came to prey on his mind, he felt like a limp rag.

He went out to tidy up the hayrick, since it would be no good going to his mother's house till much later on. About half past eight Geini turned up in a state of some agitation.

'Where's Ifan?' were her first words to Jane.

'He's out tidying the rick,' she said quietly, her eyes hooded by their lids. 'He's just doing something to kill time. He's going to go up there before long.'

Geini saw that the storm had begun to break.

'Is he going there to see about Sioned?'

'Yes.'

'It's about her that I've come.'

'Have you heard the story about her then?'

'What story?'

'That she's meeting some boy in Ceunant Forest.'

'Oh, so that's the secret, is it?'

'So you didn't know about it?'

'No, all I know is that she comes to the house very late, treats me like dirt, and gets money from Mam. I've had just about enough of it. But I'm not putting up with it any longer. Eben and I are going to get married.'

'Geini!'

At that, Ifan came in.

'Don't you think I've waited long enough already?'

'Yes you have, so long that it's a bit of a shock to hear the news. What will your mother do?'

'Only what everyone's mother has to do. I've reached the end of my tether.'

60

Ifan sighed. Trouble heaped upon trouble.

'Have you told Mam?' was his question.

'No I haven't; you can break the bad news to her, before you fetch Sioned from there.'

'No, no, I can't do it, and that's that. What I've got in mind to say about Sioned is quite enough.'

'You might as well throw my news in at the same time.'

Geini laughed, and the other two stared at her in astonishment at her flippant attitude.

'Now then,' said Geini, 'get on with you, sooner you go, sooner you get it over with.'

Geini knew her brother well. Life had seemed to her for a long time simply a matter of getting things over with, and once you'd got over one trial, there would surely be another just waiting to trip you up.

As they approached Y Fawnog, Ifan was feeling as he often did as he got closer to his old home. He felt just like he did tonight when he had been out courting, like a child afraid of being told off by his mother. He always felt that his mother was ready to pounce like a cat upon him, and she was invariably in a bad mood whenever he went out courting.

'Here's a stranger,' were his mother's first words.

And that was true. He rarely went to his mother's house except during the hay harvest and the potato picking time. The house was the same as it always was. The only thing that ever changed there was the oilcloth on the table or the matting on the floor. There was the round stone that someone had brought from the seaside one time and had been painted black and placed in the corner of the low garden wall. It lay there like some eternal sign; Ifan's gaze used to be drawn to it whenever he opened the door latch on a night of courting. Even since he married he would look for it whenever he went to Y Fawnog. It was there tonight as it always was, and as he walked past it he had exactly the same feelings as he'd had hundreds of times before he was a married man. It was really the same old story this time, except that it was somebody else's courting antics instead of his own.

Ifan plunged straight in at the deep end. 'Where's Sioned?'

'She's working late, isn't she?'

'Yes, so she says and so you say.'

'Who says different?'

'The people who've seen her with some boy in Ceunant Forest.'

His mother's face fell, and she went to sit by the fire, fiddling with the hem of her shawl.

'Who are these "people" then?' was her next question.

'Well, Morris Ifan was the one who told me.'

His mother fell silent. She had a grudging respect for the man who married her son's former lover. She continued to fiddle with her shawl. She felt a fierce indignation inside that her granddaughter had deceived her. But somewhere in the depths of her consciousness she felt that someone else, not Sioned, was really to blame. For once in her life she couldn't say what she felt.

In the meantime, Geini had been moving around between the bedroom and the kitchen, taking off her hat and coat, and putting on an apron. By this time she had come to sit on a chair drawn up to the table, and she tried to gesture towards Ifan to make him tell their mother her news.

Seeing his mother so silent, Ifan thought she must be

feeling sad, and he couldn't for the life of him hurt her more by telling her Geini's news. Talk about a hard spot! Yes, it was Hell for Ifan. This was worse than the time of his own wedding, when Geini had had to break the news to their mother for him. And now here was Geini unable to break the news about her wedding. Evidently it was easier to speak about somebody else's marriage rather than your own. But Sioned Gruffydd piped up,

'I'm afraid that you don't treat the girl right at home.'

'Not treat her right? She doesn't get treated any differently than anyone else.'

'You keep the poor girl down.'

Geini couldn't help herself.

'I'd say that she gets far too much of her own way.'

'No one was talking to you.'

'No, that's too true,' said Geini, 'no one wants to talk to me. But *I've* got a finger in this pie too. I'm not going to wait around any longer getting under the feet of you and Sioned. Do you know', she said, turning to Ifan, 'it's not because she sneaks out to go courting that I'm angry with Sioned, but because she gives herself such airs and graces, and turns her nose up at me, and I've been enough of a damned fool to run around at her beck and call like a little maid. But,' she added, turning to her mother, her voice shaking, 'everything comes to an end, and I'll be leaving here to go and get married in three weeks' time.'

'Good riddance to you,' said her mother.

'Mam!,' said Ifan, 'you should be ashamed of saying such a thing to someone who's been so good to you.'

'Huh,' said Geini, in tears, 'that's nothing to what she'll be saying to me soon.'

Ifan felt wretched. On the one hand, he felt closer to

Geini than anyone else in the world, apart from his wife and children, and his relationship with her was something different from the one he had with them. And because of that, perhaps one of the most painful wounds he received in his life was hearing his beloved sister running down his own child to his face. For Ifan, life, especially family relations, was getting more complicated every minute.

In the middle of the weeping and the rowing, Sioned came in. There was no need for her to ask what was the matter. She looked like a trapped wild bird, and her father and Geini noticed that. Ifan looked at his daughter as if he was meeting her for the first time. She was like an unknown child to him. He had never realized she was so good-looking. She had grown from a child to a young woman without his noticing.

'You'd better come home with me,' he said to her.

She could do nothing other than obey that voice.

The father and daughter did not exchange a word on their way back to Ffridd Felen, and there was not much to say when they arrived there either. Ifan was a man unable to chastise anyone, and his wife felt by now that Sioned had been punished enough by being caught. Her mother's greatest regret was that Sioned had stirred up this disagreement between Geini and Sioned Gruffydd which could turn into a breach between Geini and herself. One of the most precious things in Jane's life since coming to live in the neighbourhood was Geini's true friendship. She didn't hesitate to say this to her daughter. Ifan was glad that his wife was able to give Sioned the talking-to that he couldn't, and glad too that she focused on the pain that Sioned had caused her aunt Geini. Ifan often felt quite annoyed by his wife, but she had in her some firmness and

64

sense of justice that he couldn't help admiring – these were the things that had first drawn him to her and they remained the things he liked in her until the day he died.

Sioned herself did not say a word, a fact which curtailed her mother's sermon. But she burst out crying after a while, and consented to eat her supper.

However, no one knew the reason for her tears. She remained like the doll in the glass case in the parlour.

9

Geini got married and she and her husband went to live in a small house without land which was closer to Ffridd Felen than to Y Fawnog. Eben, her husband, had the reputation of being neat and methodical, and Geini started on her married life free from any debt to the world. She did have to borrow money from Jane and Ifan to buy her wedding clothes, but she paid them straight back afterwards.

The only thorn in Geini's side when she married was her mother. Nevertheless, she felt that the step she had taken had done her more good than anything else in her life, and that she had lived more in the past month than she had ever done before. But she still felt that she hadn't done her duty by her mother. She would feel that way for some time. For twenty years and more, she had debated, misunderstood, and rowed with her mother constantly, and in her daydreams she had pictured the day when she would leave Y Fawnog and in doing so getting the upper hand over her mother. She imagined seeing herself as the victor, placing a foot on the enemy's body. Now here was the longed-for day dawning and it was completely different from the way she had imagined it. The victory was not Geini's, for her mother looked as if she couldn't care less, though if she had looked as if she cared, that would have made it much harder for Geini to leave her, so the victory was her mother's whichever way. Although it meant that the old woman would have to start bothering with cows and pigs once more, she did not acknowledge that that was a bad thing. If she were completely honest with herself, her greatest loss was the loss of someone to put the blame on. Her meat and drink was to argue and to go on believing in her own perfection.

As for Sioned her granddaughter, after finishing her apprenticeship she got a job as a seamstress in a shop in town. Her mother had no choice but to come to terms with that. The only other option would be for her to start a sewing business herself, from home, and the job in the town seemed to Jane Gruffydd the lesser of two evils. After all, Elin was already there to help keep an eye on her. Because of her long hours, Sioned had to get lodgings in town during the week. The effect of this on Sioned was that she was much more cheerful when she did come home at weekends.

Owen started to attend the County School. Since in those days there was no transport at that time in the morning, he had to walk the four miles to School every day. He had plenty of company, since many young lads went in to work in shops and offices. They started out at the same time to the minute every morning, and everyone met at the various crossroads. If they passed the house of one of their company, they would whistle before reaching the house, and the next moment he would be out by the gate to meet them. This was the most perfect community that Owen was to encounter throughout his life. There was some unspoken understanding among them all. No one talked about it, but it was there all the same. They rarely fell out, though there would be some heated debate sometimes, such as about Disestablishment* (Owen tended to side with the church) or about the war in South Africa. But they were all of one mind when it came to other groups of people who walked the same road as them. They never joined forces with the girls who also walked into the Schools and shops of the town. They tended to look down on them, and yet they silently approved of them too. They would always have a telling or witty jibe for the troop of people who walked, in the opposite direction, from the town with goods to sell – tinned food, herrings, linen, fruit – and the troop, in their turn, would respond in kind. They were united in their approbation or disapproval of other classes of people.

They certainly disapproved of the town boys of Caernarfon, or 'Cofis' as they were called, and the latter returned their disapproval by calling them 'country bumpkins'. To the townies, the country lads were ignorant, especially of good manners, while to the country boys the townies were affected and more like girls than proper boys. There was no disagreement about these 'truths' among the group of lads that Owen was going to be a part of for the next four years. They were unanimous in their opinion of the town lads.

Owen forgot many of the things that happened to him in the County School, but he never forgot anything about any of the boys who accomanied him on the walk to School every morning. There was Richard Allt Ddu, for instance, a boy who tiptoed along at all times. He wore trousers which came down considerably below his knees, since he had younger brothers and a thrifty mother; the trousers looked loose as if he wasn't wearing any pants underneath. He never wore an overcoat, and yet he never seemed cold. He always had a mischievous smile on his face. He was the ringleader of all the fun in every children's meeting in chapel, and indeed of every other children's event. For every literary competition he would devise a humorous pseudonym, such as 'One who's out for the judges' blood', 'Hairy Hedgehog' – such pseudonyms sometimes cost him the prize. Then there was John Twnt i'r Mynydd, a harmless boy, who was naughty without meaning to be, who would extend his morning ablutions well into his hair, so that there was water dripping from the peak of his cap, and a wet lock of hair dripping down beneath it. And there was Bob Parc Glas, a quiet, neat boy with red cheeks and white skin, contributing little to the conversation, but laughing a lot.

Owen's life in the County School was quite monotonous. He hated the first weeks, when he was trying to get his tongue around the English language when he spoke to the teachers, and the English of the proper English people was very hard to understand. He never really got to like the School, but he didn't hate it any more either. When he went home at night he felt out of place, but then he was also out of place in School and away from home. He had so much homework to do when he got home that he could no longer carry out the household chores that had been his when he was at Primary School. And so, apart from the little he got at weekends, the smells of the cowshed and the hayshed become unfamiliar to him. He didn't belong either at home or at School. He excelled in every subject at School, and he was near the top of the form in everything.

Two major things happened to him while he was at

School, things which influenced him more than the education he gained there – his courtship with Gwen, Dolly Rhyd Garreg's daughter, and his friendship with Twm, his brother.

Gwen was in the same class as him, having entered without a scholarship, but winning a half-scholarship later on. Early on in his new life Owen noticed a girl who sat in the front row and who would turn around to look at him quite often. She had lively blue eyes; short, brown, curly hair and a high colour in her cheeks always. She was short and a bit plump.

One midday, when Owen was loitering in the playground after lunch, she came up to him and asked,

'Have you done your sums for tomorrow?'

'Yes,' said Owen.

'Did you manage to work out the last one?'

'Yes.'

'I couldn't work it out at all.'

And, taking her rough exercise book out from behind her back somewhere, she showed him where her difficulty lay.

Owen explained it to her, and she worked out the sum for herself straight away.

'Is it in Ffridd Felen that you live?'

'Yes.'

'I think my mam and dad know your father well.'

'Do they?'

'Well, you see, my dad is the Steward in the quarry.'

'Oh.'

And that was all Owen could say. He had never heard his father say much at all about the Steward, so that he wasn't able to feel any respectable awe in the presence of his daughter.

After this Gwen would come and pester him all the time with her homework problems, and even went so far as to walk home with him one evening, instead of taking the train home as she usually did. Bron Llech, where she lived, was on the main road, and there was a railway station there. But she never did that again. The other lads started to tease him, so he had to tell her to stop. She kept away from him for a while, but not for long. She had a way with her. She would look at him so as to suggest that it wasn't the help she got from him that counted but that he himself was the main attraction for her.

One day, as they leant on a windowsill, Owen spent ages trying to explain some difficult point to her. All the time he did so, she had a smile of contentment on her face, and Owen felt that he could take credit for giving her pleasure with his kindness. When she went to join her girl-friends in the field Owen heard them guffawing with laughter, and he saw Gwen handing around a packet of sweets. He felt hurt, and said to himself that she could at least have offered him one. If he had been nearer the group of girls he would have heard them say:

'You *are* lucky, Gwen, getting the lads to help you *and* give you sweets.'

And he would not have heard Gwen contradict them, either.

In the prize-giving day at School, Owen came first in most subjects. He took the invitation, which was embossed in English on a gold-edged card, home to his parents. But since they weren't able to understand the English, it was tossed to one side. As the days went by, the children talked about who was intending to come to the prize-giving, and

71

he got to hear that Gwen's mother was going to attend. That night he asked his mother if she were going to come along.

'Me?' she said, 'what would I do in such a place, and me not understanding a word of English?'

'Gwen's mother is coming,' said Owen.

'And she doesn't know a word of English', said his father.

'Perhaps, but she's got smart clothes, and she won't have to make any speeches.'

'Come on, Mam', said Owen, 'I'm going to be getting more prizes than anybody.'

'No, I won't come.'

When the day dawned Owen was very agitated and lonely. He felt that a prize-giving ceremony, with all its pomp, was something for 'posh people'. He was afraid of tripping as he went up to the stage, and he felt that if some of his family were there at least he would have some support behind him. As he collected his prizes, though, there was enthusiastic applause and cheering.

Afterwards, people milled around in the foyer, and Owen noticed Gwen standing beside her mother and some other girls. Gwen had won a prize for doing reasonably well in every subject and the group of girls around her were admiring the book she had received. When Gwen saw Owen, she turned her head away, but Owen noticed that one of the women, who looked very much like Gwen, was trying to keep one eye on him and the other on the general admiration that Gwen and her prize were getting. She was wearing a sateen coat and a veil. Owen didn't understand why Gwen had looked away and why she didn't bring her mother over to meet him (he took it that the woman in the sateen coat was her mother). But he convinced himself that she hadn't seen him.

The next day she was perfectly cheerful as usual in School. But after that Owen didn't take much notice of her, and kept as clear of her as he could.

The girls and boys had been in separate classes until now, but in the fourth year they were placed together in the same class once more.

By this time Gwen had got another boy to help her, and Owen felt a little jealous. He didn't want to help her himself, but he was reluctant to let anyone else take his place in Gwen's regard. He began to look on this other boy as someone who was trespassing on his property. He soon found himself talking to Gwen again, instead of avoiding her.

One Saturday afternoon in early May there was a children's Singing Festival in one of the chapels of Bron Llech. This festival was held annually in one of three neighbouring chapels. As well as singing, there were also prizes to be had for Scripture Examinations and special subject quizzes. To the younger children, being allowed to go to this festival was something like being allowed to go to town for the first time. They never left their own villages except when they went to town at Whitsun or Ascension Thursday, or to the seaside in August. The older children were much more blasé about the festival, having lost their initial excitement about it. They had become accustomed to going to new places, and Owen had got used to winning prizes. Other people also got used to seeing him win.

'There's no point in anyone else having a go; Ifan Y Fawnog's son wins every time.'

And by this time another of Ifan Y Fawnog's sons was beginning to win all the prizes in the younger age category.

The only thrill of pleasure Owen got from it now was

the thrill of seeing crowds of children all together, most of them strangers to one another, singing in harmony. A big crowd always gave him this shiver of pleasure. This particular Saturday it was hotter than usual. The chapel windows were open so that a light breeze and the bleating of sheep wafted in from the mountainside. As he looked out of the window, which he did often, Owen saw the tip beside the quarry, which glittered bluish-red in the sunshine. The sunlight fell on one ridge of rock which refracted it in all directions, like the lamplight in the chapel in winter. He felt drawn to the light. The quiz questions droned on in the background of his consciousness, while the light shining on the slate became the focus of his attention. He returned to the world of the festival when they sang 'Jesus' Flowers' or 'Faithful Soldiers'. But after they had sat down, his gaze was drawn to the slate outside once more. Then he got lost in his own little world, the light and everything else lost in his consciousness.

He soon became aware that there was a face between him and the window which was turning to look at him constantly. When he realized that, he gave himself a shake, and found that he ought to recognize that face. She smiled straight at him, and he realized that it was Gwen. She was wearing a grey-blue dress – the colour of a cuckoo – with a lace collar. Her straw hat was cream-coloured, with a garland of blue flowers around its crown. It had a wavy brim which half-shadowed her face. That was why he hadn't recognized her at first, but from then on he concentrated his gaze upon her until the end of the service, and her appearance gave him feelings which he had never had about her before. Trying to make it seem as natural as possible, he loitered in front of the chapel instead of going straight home. When Gwen came out she left the other girls

74

she was with and came up to him.

'Hello.' she said.

'Hello.' he replied shyly, rubbing the toe of his boot in the ground and creating a furrow there.

'Are you going home with those girls?' he said then. At this there came a voice from the group of girls,

'Gwen, are you coming?'

'No, I'm not coming for a while. You go on, I'll catch you up.'

It was getting dark by this time, and the people milling around the front of the chapel were all strangers to one another.

'Can I walk you home?' asked Owen.

'I don't mind,' she said, and it was her turn now to look down.

'Let's go through the fields,' said Gwen.

'You can tell me the way,' he said.

He was too shy to help her over the stiles. In the darkness everything looked like a shadow of itself, and since the paths were unfamiliar to him he felt that he was moving through a world of shadows.

'This way,' Gwen kept saying, leading him onwards, and she finally caught hold of his arm. He was not sorry that she did so. Turning towards her and looking at her face in the darkness, Owen thought that he had never seen anyone more beautiful. To tell the truth, Gwen was not beautiful. She had all the attributes of beauty – lively blue eyes, curly brown hair, a straight nose, a shapely mouth, good teeth and a clear skin. And yet she was not beautiful. It was as if someone had taken pretty pieces from a picture and had failed to put them together properly to make a whole portrait. Tonight, though, looking at her face in the darkness, with the rim of her hat in waves half-hiding it, Owen felt that she was very beautiful. He enjoyed feeling the fabric of her dress on his arm and breathing in her scent.

'You look pretty in that hat,' Owen said.

'Do you mean that? It's a very expensive hat.'

'Why do you let that townie show you how to work out the sums?'

'You didn't seem very keen to help me.'

'Well, I will from now on.'

After they reached the road, Gwen said,

'You'd better go back now, in case someone sees us. You can go this way. Keep straight on, then turn left once you get to the mountain.'

Owen turned to go. He wanted to kiss her, but he was too shy.

'Will you come and meet me somewhere next Saturday, about eight?'

'Yes, I'll come,' she said, and then disappeared because she had heard a footstep.

Owen ran home, and he wasn't much later than Twm or Bet.

Because he was carrying a lot of prizes, and because he was considered to be a steady, civil lad, no one asked any questions. But Owen was head over heels in love.

Every Saturday night for months after that they would meet in Wern Woods, halfway between their two houses. They were luckier than Sioned and Dic Edwards had been. The first time they met Owen was disappointed. Gwen had brought the everlasting sums with her.

'Oh, never mind about those,' Owen said, 'let's talk.'

For a whole week she rose up in front of his eyes as he did his Schoolwork. He would do a bit of work and then

76

fall to thinking about her. He didn't really feel like working. He couldn't get her out of his mind. His fever was calmed a little at School, since she was in the same room as him, but when he went home he would chew first his pencil and then his nails, and in his mind he would conjure up the next Saturday's meeting. Perhaps it was the night itself and its new experience which obsessed him most, and not Gwen herself. And now the longed-for night had come without mishap, and he had told a lie about the reason for going out. But he had not imagined that Gwen would bring her homework with her. This night was different from any other. But Gwen took no notice whatever of his disappointment. She was like a brand new ball, bouncing up again after being struck lightly.

'Just these two sums; we can talk afterwards.'

Owen gave in.

'There you go. Now throw the flipping book away'.

She did so, smiling like one who has got her own way.

The two talked to each other shyly, idly picking blades of grass and fern from the ground and scattering them all over the clearing.

'Where's the hat you had on last Saturday night?' asked Owen.

'Well, I'm not allowed to wear my best hat every night, you know. Why?'

'You looked so amazingly pretty in it.'

'Don't you like this one?'

'Oh yes, but the other one was exceptional.'

Gwen looked contented but not particularly gratified. Owen didn't notice the difference.

'Do you think I'm nice-looking?' was her next question.

77

'Oh yes, very nice-looking.'

'Do you know, the girls of Form Four have a game of telling the truth to one another's faces.'

'Oh! What for?'

'To stop us thinking too much of ourselves.'

'Go on with you, I'd imagine that *you'd* get to think more of yourself after that.'

'No indeed; I was really hurt'.

'Why?'

'Well, they told me that I wasn't pretty apart from my clothes.'

'Well, they told you lies, then.'

And the cold, gratified smile reappeared on her face.

And so they spent the rest of the evening and others like it, and after the sun went down, they would embrace and kiss. But Gwen would bring her School books with her every Saturday, so that Owen found himself in the position of both teacher and lover.

When the holidays came they carried on meeting in the same way, and Gwen had no excuse to bring her books with her; but she did fret about the exam results. Would she have passed? When Owen appeared uninterested, she would sigh and say that he could afford to be so nonchalant, since he was sure to have passed.

'No, I'm not so sure. But it's pointless worrying about it now. Let's talk about something else.'

But when he suggested that, he had not expected what followed.

'Tell me,' said Gwen, 'what sort of person is William your brother?'

'How do you mean, what sort of person?'

'Is he nasty or hard to live with?'

'I don't know. I don't see much of him except for when we go to bed, and he's always too tired to talk much there. Why do you ask?'

'Oh, nothing,' she said, 'but I hear dad talk about him sometimes to my mother.'

'Does he say anything bad about him?'

'Oh no, nothing, just that your dad and he are excellent workers.'

This silenced Owen. The relationship that Gwen's father had with his brother and father had never even dawned on Owen before.

So the weeks passed, and the day of the exam results came ever closer. Owen worried that his courtship with Gwen had interfered with his work. But when Saturday night came around he forgot those worries.

The prize-giving was in October. As usual, Owen brought the gold-rimmed invitation card home to his father and mother, and as usual Jane Gruffydd tossed it to one side on the table.

'No, you've got to come this time,' said Owen.

'Yes, you go, Jane,' said Ifan, 'fair play to the boy. You might as well.'

'Yes, please come, mam; I got the best certificate in the exam'.

This was the first time they had heard of this. They had been unable to understand the official English report that came by post, and Owen hadn't bothered to translate it.

'I don't have enough English or clothes to come,' said Jane Gruffydd.

'You don't need any English,' said Owen, 'everyone will be speaking Welsh except for those up on the stage.'

'Yes, and go and order yourself a coat from the tailor,'

said Ifan, 'and you can take Ann Ifans with you for company.'

And so it turned out. From his seat at the front of the stage Owen could see his mother and Ann sitting in the middle of the audience. He had never seen his mother in a coat before, only in a dress, or with a cape on. She looked handsome, and she was wearing a new black toque with a purple flower on it, instead of the bonnet that she had worn for years. She had a white lace cravat around her neck, with a big black brooch as a fastener. As he went up to collect his prizes, Owen felt happier, if more agitated, because his mother was there. His consciousness was full of the presence of his mother and Ann, and yet he had not forgotten about Gwen. When her turn came to go and collect her certificate, Owen was struck by how half-hearted the applause was in comparison with that received by many of the other girls. Nor did she receive a very good certificate. Owen felt quite sorry for her. But she looked very grand, in a dress of braid-trimmed white alpaca with just a touch of colour in it.

He was glad to see the end of the ceremony. He never liked the feel of the School on prize-giving day – the palm trees on the stage, everyone in their best clothes, and the snobbishly genteel atmosphere which filled the whole place.

When the children gathered together at the end to see one another's prize books, Owen went to talk to Gwen.

'You've got a posh dress on,' he said, to avoid talking about the prizes.

But this time she didn't cheer up.

'My father and mother are here,' she said, 'and I have to go and be with them.'

'My mother's here too,' he said, 'with a friend of hers.'

Gwen looked as astounded as if she were hearing for

the first time that he even had a mother.

'Oh?' she said, and disappeared in the direction of her family.

Of all the 'Ohs' that Owen ever heard in his life, that one was the most expressive. He never heard one, either before or after, so full of mocking surprise.

Later on he stood in the lobby, close to the front door, with his mother and Ann Ifans. He saw Gwen and her parents coming towards them on their way out. This time it was impossible for Gwen not to have seen him. He remembered the first prize-giving ceremony, when she had failed to see him. He stood this time, looking straight at them. But the three went past them, pretending not to notice their presence.

'Hang on a minute,' said Ann Ifans, 'wasn't that Dolly Rhyd Garreg and her husband?'

'Yes,' said Jane Gruffydd.

'Was that their daughter?'

'Yes,' said Owen, almost choking.

'What a stuck-up little madam, isn't she?' said Ann Ifans, 'and she had fewer cheers than anyone else.'

This comment made them laugh, and Owen at least was grateful for it.

Owen now stayed in town during the winter, since his work was becoming more demanding. The three of them went to his lodgings for tea. Owen felt the most extraordinary mixture of emotions tearing at his insides. Disappointment, indignation, happiness. Disappointment and indignation on account of Gwen's behaviour, and happiness because of his mother's being there. He was brave enough to forget about Gwen's scorn over tea, and concentrate all his attention on his mother and making her happy. He was in a period of his life when everything hurt him. Seeing his mother and Ann Ifans take such pleasure in something as simple as a lodging house tea and attending a prize-giving ceremony made him feel rather sad.

'Those people in the black capes, they were the teachers, were they, Owen?' asked Ann Ifans.

'Yes, they've all got either a B.A. or a B.Sc.'

'Gosh, aren't they lucky. You'll be like them one day,' she said, admiringly.

'I don't know, indeed.'

'And perhaps that girl of Dolly's will get one too,' said Jane Gruffydd, with no hint of admiration.

'No, she won't, I hope,' said Ann Ifans. But, thinking about it, of course she won't, because God knows full well who to give a B.A. to.'

Owen almost choked with laughter.

'I wish I could have understood what that man who was giving out the prizes was saying,' said Jane Gruffydd, 'didn't he look like a nice man? Did he give a good speech, Owen?'

'Yes.'

'Isn't it a shame we don't understand a bit of English, Ann Ifans?'

'I don't know, indeed; you understand quite enough in this old world as it is. Who knows how much pain you manage to avoid by not knowing English?'

Owen and Jane Gruffydd laughed heartily.

'How long is it since you were in town before, Jane Gruffydd?'

'Not since the day we took the pigs for weighing, but I never really count that; it's been more than a year since I was here with time to have a proper look around.'

'I'm sure Owen here will take us for a ride in a closed carriage when he starts earning,' said Ann Ifans.

'Alright,' said Owen, drinking in the spirit of the conversation, 'the first pay packet I get, we'll go for a trip to Anglesey.'

'Let's go to the Lleyn Peninsula.'

'Yes, to Lleyn, then.'

And a look of joy tinged with sadness came to Jane Gruffydd's face.

'Lots of things will happen before then, I expect,' she said.

But Owen was certain that she was happy at that moment. She had obviously enjoyed her day. Owen watched her as she got up to leave, tall and dignified in her new coat, her black hair sweeping in waves over her ears under her new hat, and more than anything that spiritual calm that was always such an essential part of her presence.

Owen couldn't help comparing her to Gwen's mother, who was short and fat, and wore a sateen coat which made her look fatter still, and the veil that made her face look less common.

They called in with Sioned at the shop for a minute. Sioned was shy, but tried her best to be nice. Elin was clearly very glad to see them, and she threw off her apron and cap in order to come and walk part of the way home with them.

The crows cawed in Afon Wood, and through the trees poured the colour of an October sunset, a fiery orange which rippled on the surface of the river. The hills and quarries looked dark and sad. There was a wintry nip in the air.

It had been a strange evening for Owen – accompanying his mother home – not going the whole way

– having to turn back. He felt stupidly tender-hearted. He turned around many times to wave to his mother.

'What's the matter with you?' said Elin.

He didn't answer.

'Come in with me for a bit,' she said.

'No, not tonight; I'll come tomorrow if that's alright.'

He returned to his lodgings, went to his room and cried.

Then he went downstairs again, and played dominoes with his landlord for hours.

In his bed that night, Owen turned over in his mind the affair with Gwen right from the start and he began to realize what a fool he had been to see anything in her in the first place. He could read her like a book now. He could see her selfishness quite clearly. He was glad that he had woken up to it now, before anyone else heard about their courtship. That was a good thing. As far as he knew, nobody was aware of the relationship. There had been enough of a fuss in Ffridd Felen when Sioned was found out doing the same thing. The feeling that overwhelmed him in his bed that night was shame, shame that he had been so foolish over Gwen, and so underhand to his parents, and the greatest shame was that it had been done and there was no going back on it, something that no one can bear to think of. All this turned to a feeling of hatred in his heart, and made him more determined, like someone who had emerged from the cauldron having been cleansed. He could leave it all behind him without regret. It had been an experience, a bitter one at present, but in years to come, within the pattern of his whole life, it would take up only a small place.

He thought at first of sending a note to Gwen on the following day, but recalling some of her comments about his family, and her references to his parents in Ffridd

Felen, it occurred to him that sending a written note could do his family harm, though it might do Gwen, and his own conscience, a lot of good. By this time, though, he didn't feel that Gwen was worth the trouble of writing a long accusation.

He saw her during the dinner hour. She came up to him with that gratified smile of hers which he now hated. Calmly he said to her,

'Since neither I nor my family were good enough for you yesterday, I'm not good enough for you today, nor will I ever be again.'

Having uttered the words, he ran away from her, leaving her standing there in astonishment. She was going to answer him, but she didn't get a chance. And that was the end of Owen Ffridd Felen's first love affair.

10

For the next two years in the County School nothing occupied Owen's mind except his work; and he couldn't understand how it could ever have been otherwise.

In his last year, Twm started in the County School, having also won a scholarship, and since Owen was already lodging in town, their parents thought it would be best for Twm to lodge there too so that Owen could keep an eye on him. Ifan and Jane Gruffydd always thought that some of their children could keep an eye on the others, and in this way they could rid themselves of some of the responsibility of parenthood. Neither of them could ever be called a disciplinarian. The children were like them in this, and so they never discharged their duties of 'keeping an eye on' their siblings. Owen had enough to do to keep his eye on his Latin and Greek. But he couldn't help but notice Twm when he was actually in the same lodging house as him. He couldn't do otherwise. Twm was actually an exceptionally handsome boy – similar to Sioned his sister in looks, but more genial and open in his ways. When

Owen had passed the exam to get into the County School, Twm had been just a little whippersnapper of seven, trotting around everywhere with his sister Bet, so that Owen had not really known him as well as the other children.

All kinds of Schoolwork was child's play for Twm. He was a feather of a child, floating past everyone so lightly that no one really noticed him. He did his homework in a few minutes, then sat in a chair, whistling.

'Get on with your work,' said Owen.

'I've finished it,' said Twm.

'You can't have finished it so quickly. Let me see.'

And Twm, still whistling, and tipping his chair back nonchalantly, would pass him his exercise book. Owen found that it was all done correctly.

'Look, you need to get some books from the library, so that you have something to read.'

'I'd rather go out.'

'Well, go on then, for tonight, but don't be too long.'

In about two hours Twm returned, smelling of the chip shop.

'Where have you been?'

'Down to the harbour with the lads and afterwards in the chip shop.'

'What lads?'

'The town lads, those in the same class as me. Davey and Arthur.'

And that's how things went most of the time from then on. Twm enjoyed himself in the town. Owen never saw him. The lodging house was just a waiting room for Owen to do his homework in, and he himself never went out. He never really got accustomed to the heavy atmosphere of a town

87

house, an atmosphere he always associated with dangling sticky paper for catching flies in late September. Houses with their closed, garden-less backs to each other, and their clothes lines outside weighed down with grimy washing. But before Twm had been in the town a couple of months he already knew where the best chip shop was, where to get cheap windfall apples, where every back lane led to, and where the best hiding places were in the harbour. He knew every town boy in the School, and every madman and odd character who used to loiter on street corners and in the marketplace. Owen was left in peace to do his homework, and since Twm always did his own, he wasn't bothered.

Sometimes Twm went along to Revival* meetings, more out of curiosity than anything else. He managed to get Owen to go too once or twice, but Owen was really not interested in them, and he had by this time managed to keep himself and his work quite separate from the world outside. Twm went to the Revival meetings regularly for a while and then grew tired of them. But he told Owen funny stories about what had happened there sometimes.

He started visiting Elin at her place as well, and had supper with her, and often money for his supper in the chip shop on the following evening. Twm was more of an unknown brother to Elin even than to Owen, and as such Elin delighted in him as in a new discovery. She got out of him every story he knew about home and about Owen, yes, and about Sioned. In his wanderings around town after closing time, Twm often came across Sioned, all dressed up, walking out with some boy or other. Through his friends he found out that he was a town boy, a clerk in one of the shops. He told Elin these stories enthusiastically, because talking about Sioned closed the gap of estrangement between them, and because he liked talking and took an interest in other people's lives. When Elin had her night off on Saturdays Sioned would be working late, and she would walk home or take the last brake, so Elin never saw her, and though she urged her to come and visit her at her place, Sioned never did. So, Twm's news about Sioned was of interest to Elin.

'What did he look like, Twm?' she said.

'Some hobbledehoy of a chap,' said Twm. 'Hobbledehoy' might not have meant much to most people, but it told Elin all she wanted to know.

'It would be much better for Sioned to go out with quarry-lads, instead of going for milksops like that. She'll find out one day that these townies are no match for her.'

'Or that she's no match for them,' said Twm.

'Don't you be so sure,' said Elin, '*Comic Cuts* is about the deepest thing that most of them can understand.'

After going back to his lodgings, Twm told Owen everything, including Elin's remarks. They talked while lying in bed since the landlady didn't approve of wasting lamp oil.

'Don't you say anything about this at home,' said Owen.

'Do you really think I would be daft enough to say anything?' said Twm, hurt.

'Well, alright, I was just giving you a bit of a reminder, because there's already been one big fuss over Sioned at home.'

'What was that?'

And as he told his brother the story about Sioned in the darkness, Owen felt that he was beginning to get to know his little brother better.

Recalling the derision heaped on him by the lads like

Sioned's boyfriend who used to walk into town, Owen couldn't help saying, 'She's a damned fool.'

'But the town lads aren't all like that,' said Twm.

'Even if they were like angels, they're still different from us,' said Owen.

Within the year, Owen went to College in Bangor on a twenty-pound scholarship, with the intention of training to be a teacher. Only one other thing was thought to be suitable for him, and that was to be a preacher. But that didn't run in the Ffridd Felen family, and Owen had never been drawn in that direction. For three years afterwards Twm had to walk all the way home rather than lodge in the town, a fact which made him very sad at first.

11

Back home, Jane and Ifan Gruffydd kept on trying to make ends meet. By this time wages at the quarry were lower than they had ever been, and the cost of living much higher. William grew to an age when he was able to pay for his own food rather than give all his wages to his mother, a fact which gave him more independence and made her poorer. He got his food and laundry and a number of other little things for thirty shillings a month. The hard fact for William was that his wages were actually going down as he grew older, and he was unable to save any of his money. This made him discontented and quarrelsome. Things were made even worse for him and his father because of the attitude of the Steward and his deputy, the Little Steward, towards them. The market for slate was in a poor state because the building industry was very sluggish and because slate was being imported from abroad. Although wages were low generally, everyone's wages were not as low as those of Ifan and William, since there was a great deal of toadying to the officials going on – many a chicken and goose appearing on the Steward's table of a Sunday had been in a quarryman's field the weekend before. Since the family at Ffridd Felen did not use their poultry for such purposes, they didn't receive any favours. Morris Ifan, the Little Steward, preferred to do his worst rather than his best for his wife's former lover, and for the father and brother of the boy who snatched all the prizes from his daughter at School. In his own job, Morris could do little harm apart from that which his tongue could accomplish, but in his dealings with the Steward his influence reached much further.

At the start of the month, when Buckley the Steward would come around to agree a price for their work, Ifan would wince in discomfort. The rock face assigned to himself and his partners was always a poor one. It was impossible to negotiate for a better one, or beg for a better price. If the rock face and the slate were good, a low price was to be expected, but since they were otherwise, they could have expected a better price at the start of the month. But they had to be content with a low price, and they could be sure that when the market was weak the slate inspector would smash more of the slates with faults in them at the end of the month.

Ifan often brought home three pounds a month, sometimes four, and if he brought home five, he considered that a good wage. Once he brought home just eighteen shillings, having worked hard for it for a whole month.

Until now, William had been dependent on working with other men's leftover rocks,* a mode of work which was very erratic, and he had no hope of getting anything better, except to be taken on as a journeyman with one of the established gangs of men. But then a journeyman's wages were so low that he would scarcely be any better off. The only advantage would that he would have a surer idea of what his wages would be.

Jane and Ifan were unable to pay off any of the money they owed on their smallholding. Indeed, sometimes they had to mortgage it further rather than pay off some of the mortgage, when they needed a new cow, and had sold the old one for less money. They bred enough pigs to pay the interest and the rates, and although Jane Gruffydd had suggested selling three litters of pigs in a year instead of two, through buying two piglets before the two porkers had been sold, somehow or other they were no better off. The bill for the pig-meal in the shop was even more, and so was her own fatigue at the end of the day.

Owen and Twm had, it is true, won their scholarships, but because Moel Arian was so remote and far from town, it was an extra cost to pay for their lodgings there towards the end of their School careers. It would be cruel to make them walk the whole way home and then start on their homework, once that had become much more demanding. They needed better clothes, and their books were expensive. (They did get some financial help with the latter.)

William and Elin were now paying their own way – though William failed to do so some months – but Sioned did not. Her wages were not enough to keep her in food and clothing. But Jane Gruffydd was able to make plenty of clothes for Bet out of Sioned's old clothes. When the mother needed new clothes for herself, such as for the prize-giving ceremony, that meant getting into more debt in order to buy them.

She never scrimped on food, though. She never made a big effort, as some did, to take more butter to sell in the shop by putting less on the bread at home, or by mixing butter and margarine, as others did. She had one or two steady customers, and they always got their buttermilk for nothing. She worked from morning to night, housework and most of the farm work. She sewed the children's underclothes and top clothes herself. She would cut up and remake Ifan and William's old trousers in order to make pairs for Owen and Twm, before they went to the County School. She had little spare time to go anywhere, nor to read. If she put on her spectacles in the evening to read a book, she would always fall straight asleep.

Her husband was the same. He worked his fingers to the bone in the quarry; he sweated and got soaked; he would come home in winter soaked to the skin, and was too tired even to read the newspaper. In spring and summer there was always plenty to do on the farm every evening and Saturday afternoon.

The only time off they got was getting up later on a Sunday morning, and going to town sometimes on a Saturday afternoon. They didn't complain about their lack of holidays. They would not have known what to do on a holiday if they had them more often. Their fate was the pain and worry of wondering how they were going to pay their way, how to get into the clear with the world, and of getting things that they had needed all through their lives but had never been able to afford.

But after he had finished tending the potatoes or covering the hayrick, Ifan would get pleasure from leaning on the wall, having a leisurely smoke and admiring his own handiwork, sometimes by himself, sometimes with a friend of his. There was pleasure in seeing the straight rows and the virgin soil around the dark shoots of the potatoes; seeing the sides of the rick smooth and solid, and drinking in the sweet scent of the hay; or, in the quarry, getting good slate which split cleanly like gold, whipping through the work quickly, whistling all the time, and being able to chat after eating his food in the cabin at midday. Yes, life did have its pleasures.

And in the evening, putting his foot up on the low wall in front of the house, and letting his gaze rest on the blush of the waves as the sun set, before he turned back to the house to have his supper, a fine contentment would sweep over him.

William was different. He had not known worse times, but he had known better. That was one disadvantage of the system that allowed boys' fathers to work for them when they first went to the quarry. It gave them unrealistic ideas about what a quarryman could earn, and as he watched his own wages dwindle instead of increasing, William began to lay the blame on the only visible signs of the system, namely the stewards and the owners; and indeed perhaps they were the system. His father had known better times and worse ones. He knew what it was to start work at nine years old, carrying heavy loads of slates on his back, before his own soft bones began to harden. He knew what it was to get up at four o'clock on a Saturday morning and go to the quarry by the light of a lamp and work until one, in order to make a half day into a full one. He knew what it was to go into the quarry and dangle there by a rope when he should have been in School at his lessons, and sheer rock faces were for him only what trees are to a squirrel.

And yet, when he was the same age that William was now, he knew what it was to earn a decent wage and to dream about getting married, before his father was killed in the quarry. William had never had that pleasure. William got a taste for travelling, since there were brakes running regularly to town, and there were trains going from there to wherever you wanted to go. When his father was young, he had had to walk everywhere. This had not stopped him travelling around, but it had stopped him spending much money on it.

Evening classes in English and arithmetic were started in the village. English was a help to get on in the world, and arithmetic was a useful thing to know. There was a need to raise the worker up from his present position. He needed to be given a living wage. After learning a little more English than they were taught in Primary School, the young people began to read about the new ideas that were beginning to spread in England and South Wales. Whereas their fathers (the brightest amongst them) had learned about the ideas of Thomas Gee and S. R., the children (the brightest of them) came to learn about the ideas of Robert Blatchford and Keir Hardie.*

Some of the young people started to meet in the barber's hut, and they busied themselves in establishing a Branch of the Independent Labour Party. William was the main leader of this movement. His primary concern was trying to persuade his fellow-quarrymen to join the Quarrymen's Union. They would never get a guaranteed wage without it. In the enthusiastic knowledge of the justice of what they stood for, they felt that every quarryman would surely join up immediately. Then there would be no difficulty in standing up against any lowering of wages. Their first disappointment was seeing how lukewarm their fellow-workers were about the whole thing; some were reluctant to get into the masters' bad books, others unable to see what good would come of it, and still others completely indifferent to it all. There were few who were really committed. Some, like Ifan Gruffydd, paid their membership out of a sense of duty. They felt that it could be a good thing in the long run, in generations to come perhaps, but not in their own lifetime.

In this way, this group of youngsters in the neighbourhood came to take an interest in the Worker. They got their ideas from English books and from Welsh papers which echoed the English ones. The Worker in Wales came to be considered as being in the same boat as the Worker in England. To them it was the same problem in every country, and the enemy was the same – namely, capitalism. William read everything on this topic he could get his hands on. And as he was tussling with these problems, nobody told him that the very quarry he himself worked in had been started initially by workers themselves, who shared the profit equally.

And a change came over their religion. Their grandfathers and grandmothers, who had founded the Nonconformist chapels scattered over these hills, had been serious students of theology. Piety and self-sacrifice were the essence of their religion. Those people's grandchildren were devoid of piety, and there was not so much call for sacrifice. They continued to study theology, but as something cold and separate from themselves. They were interested in subjects such as the Person of Christ, the Incarnation, Providence, Atonement, as intellectual matters and not as ideas which were intimately related to their own lives, but in this sense the topics still had a grip on the minds of the young, as they had on the middle-aged and the old. As the circumstances of their everyday lives changed, as the world became more fragile, a change also came in their attitudes towards religion. This change was seen in the young people. To those who were committed to worker's rights, what was important now was a man's duty to his fellow-man, and the Sermon on the Mount became more important than the Epistles of St Paul. Their attitudes towards their preachers changed too. The best ministers now were those who preached social justice and men's duty to help one another. Young people were pleased when Christ was called a Socialist. But this was again a matter of interest to the intellect, and not a matter of faith. Their interest shifted from Christ the Redeemer to Christ the Example. That had no effect on their lives. They enjoyed a good sermon from the pulpit, and a good debate in Sunday School. They had no minister with whom to agree or to disagree.

Their interest in politics was one-sided. The old and the middle-aged were Radicals, because they believed that Radicalism was best for the workers. The Tory Party was the party of the 'toffs', and the primary aim of the toffs was to keep the workers down. Liberalism had gained ground ever since 1868,* and the quarrymen still referred to freedom for the worker and the standard of living. Now here was a group of young people learning to read English and reading about people who were beginning to tire of Liberalism and who were saying that the big battle of the future would be between Capital and Labour, and that Liberalism was just another name for capitalism. Their elders were a little suspicious of them, and deacons and pillars of the chapel openly frowned upon them because this new party was associated with atheism. This didn't bring family disagreements to Ffridd Felen, though, since there were no ingrained religious or political beliefs there to be undermined.

The Moel Arian Branch of the Independent Labour Party didn't grow much in numbers, and the spread of its influence was slow. But the few who were members were deeply committed. They made an effort to get new members and to persuade the quarrymen to join the Union. There were a number of small-scale strikes in the neighbourhood during these years but the men didn't come out under the aegis of the Quarrymen's Union, but of their own accord, and very few of them were supported by the Union. The terms on which wages were negotiated worsened all the time, and things didn't improve after strike action. It was useless to try to persuade the men that a minimum wage would never be got without the help of the Union. One of the men most disappointed at this state of affairs was William Ffridd Felen. He spoke and argued in favour of the new party whenever he got a chance. He managed to get people to agree with, but not to cooperate, with him. They liked his eloquence, and expressed their admiration of him in that characteristic saying of theirs: 'That William Ffridd Felen is a tough customer.' Their admiration of Lloyd George* was based on the same notion.

12

Shortly before Owen went to College, Sioned Gruffydd, Y Fawnog, died. She had a stroke and died within three days, without regaining consciousness. Geini and Eben had gone to live with her a few months after they married. The old woman had failed to cope on her own. She refused to leave Y Fawnog, though Geini offered her own house to her, and she and Eben would have gone to live in Y Fawnog. She had agreed reluctantly to have Geini and her husband come to Y Fawnog but on her own terms, not theirs. She refused to let go of the reins, so that Geini found herself once more working as her mother's maidservant. Yet she could save on paying rent, and Eben brought home quite a regular salary from the quarry because he was a carpenter. Old age or something else had mellowed Sioned Gruffydd quite a bit. She still found fault, but Geini didn't care so much about that any more. She had Eben, and she didn't have to work so hard.

Sioned Ffridd Felen had no time when she was at home at the weekend to go and see her grandmother. Since she had started working in the town, she hadn't needed a scapegoat to blame for her absences on her amorous adventures. When a message was sent to her telling of her grandmother's illness, she didn't take much notice of it. When she heard of her grandmother's death, the first thought that came into Sioned's head was: would she look good in black? And when she had persuaded herself that she would, she was pleased at the thought of getting some new clothes. She decided that she would insist on having a black dress with a white collar, and a white hat with a black ribbon around it. She ordered the dress in the shop where she worked without consulting her mother beforehand.

Elin came to her in the shop to find out what she was going to do about buying black clothes. If she managed to persuade Sioned to do the same, she was ready to dare to flout the expectations of the community and not go into mourning, but Sioned poured cold water on such an idea.

'Why not?' said Elin innocently.

'Well, just think of how people would talk about us.'

'Let them talk. It's not them who have to pay for the new clothes.'

'I don't care; I've already ordered my new suit.'

'Who's going to pay for it?'

'Whoever wants to. I'm determined to have a black suit in memory of my grandmother.'

'Yes, I remember; you used to be very fond of her, when it was worth your while.'

Sioned blushed and sailed out with her head in the air to the sewing room, where the girls who had eavesdropped on the conversation were smirking at each other.

Elin bought a black dress of the cheapest material possible, and it was made up by the cheapest seamstress in the parish.

The day of their mother's funeral was the first time many of the offspring of Y Fawnog had seen each other for years. Betsan and William were older than Ifan. Then came Gwen, Huw, Morris, Ann, Edward, and Geini. Apart from Ifan and Geini, they had all left Moel Arian and had gone to live in different parts of the county. William and Gwen lived furthest away, and it was they who were seen most rarely. But, with the exception of Betsan, none of the others bothered much about visiting their mother. They came there when they heard that she was ill, and they found fault with Geini that she hadn't done this or that. They cavilled and questioned about how she had come to have the stroke. Had someone perhaps upset or said something nasty to her? They mooched about the place exactly as they had done when Ifan had been ill, and Geini had no chance to get close to the bed. They sat at the bedside, giving their mother sips of water, or rearranging the bedding around her chin. Since Geini had to prepare food for them all there was more work for her looking after them than looking after her mother, and none of them offered to help her wash the bedclothes.

Ifan came, and sat pensively by the fire in the kitchen. He went to the bedroom from time to time and had a look at his mother, and that was all. Geini felt warmer towards him because he behaved like that. The shamelessness of the rest of them drove her mad. She tried to keep her anger in check, since she wouldn't have to do so for long. But she failed on one occasion. Ann had been sitting there like a doll in the bedroom since ten o'clock in the morning, without moving an inch except to get up to have her lunch. About three o'clock in the afternoon she got up and fetched a clean cloth from a drawer in the dresser to mop up her mother's dribbling.

'Hold on,' said Geini, 'it's my linen in that drawer; Mam's cloths are in the drawer above.'

'Oh, I didn't know that you had your own things,' said Ann, a bit shocked.

'What did you think I used when I was living in my own house, then?' said Geini.

'Your family is strange,' said Eben one night after Sioned Gruffydd had passed away, 'when your mother was alive they all kept away, except Ifan and Betsan, but once they found out that she was about to die, they were buzzing around your head like a swarm of bees, and they looked at you and me as if we were murderers.'

'You're spot on there,' said Geini. 'All of them, except Ifan and William and Betsan, have been asking whether she left a will.'

'So, has she?'

'I don't know; I'm hoping she hasn't, because it's likely that she'd leave her money to those who behaved the worst towards her.'

This was the only time that the offspring of Y Fawnog saw each other – whenever there was a funeral of someone in the family, and they were really more like strangers to one another than many of their neighbours. And unlike the next generation, they hadn't even known one another well as children, only the ones who were right next to them in age. In those days a son was sent to the quarry or a girl sent to be a maidservant at about the age of ten. They were out on their ear before they had left the hearth almost, and home was only a place from which to turn children out into the world.

Sioned Gruffydd's funeral was a cold affair. It didn't occur to any of her children not to follow the usual custom of accepting 'contributions'* from all comers, since there hadn't been a funeral in the household for twenty-five years. It was agreed that William, as the eldest son, would accept the offerings, and he sat on the settle by the fire, with a round table in front of him, a large, black-bordered handkerchief spread out on it to receive the offerings. He had left home after marrying and had gone to live in Bont-y-Braich, and so only the old and middle-aged people of the district knew him. The rest of Sioned Gruffydd's children and children-in-law sat around the walls of the kitchen. She had no brother or sister still living. The grandchildren stood around outside the door, eyeing up one another's clothes, some of them seeing their cousins for the very first time.

Inside the kitchen it was sombre and dark. The curtains at the windows of the kitchen and the bedroom didn't reach right down to the sills, so that a small amount of light seeped in there, and through the open door. The people facing the door could see a strip of light falling on the coffin in the bedroom. The women were all wearing black, and they had crepe draped around their hats; Gwen even had crepe in swags on her coat and skirt as well. From the bedroom came the smell of the pine coffin, and in the kitchen was the smell of black kid gloves. Gwen looked round every few minutes to see who was coming in, and if she didn't know them she would ask Geini in a loud voice who they were, until Geini finally told her to be quiet. Betsan had been trying to say the same thing for ages by glowering at her. People came in one by one and put their sixpences on the table. If they were of the same age as William they said,

'How are you, old boy, after all these years?'

The others turned away from the table and went back to join the crowd of people waiting outside. Sometimes there was a quiet spell when nobody came in, and in that silence you could hear the lazy whistling of the big kettle on the hob, a light patch on its side from the sunshine that came down the chimney. The sound of the kettle was so homely to Geini that she felt that she ought to just go and make some tea, as if all the funeral preparations were a dream. Then the last bunch of people came in, and in the quiet spell afterwards, the voice of the preacher gave out the hymn. At the graveside Ifan was the only one who wept. Owen looked at him, for this was the first time he had ever seen his father crying.

Shortly before the funeral the Schoolmaster had called round at Ffridd Felen to say that Sioned Gruffydd had made a will, which she had left in his keeping, since he had drawn it up for her. He had been commanded by her not to mention it until the day of her funeral, and since that was the only day when all the family was likely to be gathered together, he suggested that it would be sensible to read it out after tea. So the Schoolmaster had to come and have tea with them, and it was certainly one of the most uncomfortable meals any of them had had for many years.

And there at the table, after the crockery had been cleared away, Sioned Gruffydd's will was read out. The Schoolmaster had looked quite worried throughout the meal, since he knew that the contents of the will would please nobody. The old woman had left her money to her granddaughter, Sioned Ffridd Felen. The date on the will was October 12, 1899, which was shortly after Geini had married. The moment they heard what was in the will was a terrible one for everyone present, not excepting the Schoolmaster himself, but no one showed their feelings while he was still there. Geini went white, and Ifan began to tremble. It was the two of them who were hurt most by hearing the news. The Schoolmaster got up to leave, and William, too, said that he had to go and catch his train.

'Wait a minute,' said William, who had beads of sweat standing out like peas on his forehead. 'Is there any mention of the furniture and the farm animals and so on, Mr Evans?'

'No, nothing at all. Only the money she had in the bank.'

'Are you sure that's the last will that Mam made?'

'As far as I know, yes. Well, good day to you now.' And the Schoolmaster escaped.

'Sit down a minute,' Ifan said to William.

'What would I want to sit down for? I'd better catch my train.'

'No. You heard what the man said about the furniture.'

'I couldn't care less about the furniture.'

'But the others do care.'

'Yes,' said Ann, the feathers on her hat nodding emphatically. 'We've got to watch out that the furniture doesn't go the same way as the money.' And she glared at Ifan. All the others, apart from William, Betsan, and Geini, did the same.

'It's obvious that somebody's been pushing his children into Mam's lap, to get the money to send the children to School,' said Gwen.

It dawned on Ifan what she was thinking, and as he looked at the self-satisfied, wounded expressions on the faces of most of his family, all the injustices of his life welled up in his breast, and he burst out:

'Look here,' he said, his voice shaking, 'if you think I'm going to get a penny of that money from Sioned, my daughter, you need to think again. She's over twenty-one, and she can do whatever she likes with it, so I'm pretty sure that none of us will get any of it. If I did get my hands on it, though, it would be coming to the right place. It's my money because I earned it after father died, and I was enough of a fool to give it all, every penny more or less, to Mam, and I worked like a navvy here, while some of you were able to swagger off to town every Saturday night, and thinking that you were doing your duty just by giving a little something for your food, and all the rest you spent on clothes and beer. But what I'd really like is to see Geini have the money because she's the one who did most for Mam at the end of her life, when everyone else kept away.'

'Quite right,' said Betsan.

Ifan mopped the sweat from his forehead with his white handkerchief. That was the longest speech he had ever made in his life.

Gwen, Huw, Edward, Ann and Morris sniffed their dissent.

William put down his umbrella on a chair, indicating that he was going to miss that train and catch the next.

'So there's no mention of the furniture and the cattle?' asked William.

'No, there isn't,' said Ifan.

'It's strange that the Schoolmaster didn't enlighten her about that, since he *is* a Schoolmaster,' said Edward.

'I expect he could see that they would go the same way as the rest,' said Betsan.

'You're probably right there,' said Ifan.

'Well, I suggest,' said Betsan, 'that Geini should get all the furniture in the house and everything else that's here, the two cows, the two pigs and the hayrick and all those things. I would suggest that Ifan should get half of it, if I knew that he would get nothing from Sioned, but I'm sure she'll give some of the money to her father and mother.'

The others laughed spitefully.

Morris asked, 'Why should Geini get more than the rest of us?'

'Because she worked for it all by staying at home to look after Mam,' said Ifan, 'and none of you can claim that you did the same.'

'No, she shan't have it all indeed,' said Gwen. 'I suggest that everything here should be sold and the proceeds shared equally among us all.'

'And each of us will then get about six pounds,' said Betsan.

'That would be good enough for some of us,' said Morris, the poorest and the most impractical of them all, whose wife was as wasteful as himself, one of those who eat the bread on the day it's baked.

'Look here, William,' said Ifan, 'you're the eldest. You make the decision. You've got two suggestions now. I'm ready to go home.'

'Oh yes, I'm sure, to tell your daughter the good news,' said Gwen.

'Well,' said Geini, who had stayed as silent as a statue up to now, 'I'm not prepared to take anything unless everyone is unanimous, and so we'd better sell everything and share the money.'

And that's what was agreed upon.

In Ffridd Felen there was a tea party going on. Jane Gruffydd had gone straight home from the funeral and, in order to help Geini out, had taken all the children of the family home with her to have tea. The children were having a whale of a time, and were in awe of their Auntie Jane. While Elin and her mother sat down to have a cup of tea by the fire before Elin had to start her journey back to town, the children played in the fields, in the yard, and in every hole and corner of the byre and the sheds. They were very friendly, and thinking that they would like to see more of one another, and the children from away regarded Ffridd Felen as a first-class place to be. Sioned was upstairs admiring herself in the mirror.

Ifan Gruffydd arrived home and when he saw the children enjoying themselves together so much a lump came to his throat. He felt bad about interrupting their comradeship and telling them to go and seek out their parents in Y Fawnog.

This had been the strangest day in Ifan Gruffydd's life since the day of his father's death. That day had been a happy one in comparison with this one. Then, he had only one feeling – a feeling of longing and pity; a longing for his father, the quiet, kind man who had walked beside him every day to the quarry ever since he had started working there, and pity for his mother who had been left a widow with such a burden upon her, and a feeling too of the cruelty of fate which struck a man down in the flower of his days, without letting him reach the contentment of old age.

Today, it was different. His mother had been blessed with a long life. In her final years her attitude towards those of her children who had been good to her was impossible for Ifan to understand; she had been so selfish. She hadn't been like that when her children were younger. And as he heard her groans on her deathbed, her younger years became more vivid in Ifan's mind than the years of late – those earlier days when she worked from morning to night;

and he remembered that she, as well as his father, had been responsible for the flourishing of Y Fawnog, its transformation from poor mountain land to a productive little farm. The day before, as he was carrying slate slabs to her grave, he saw that his father's gravestone had sunk into the ground and was now small. He felt it was a strange thing to be laying down side by side the bodies of two people who had once been of the same flesh and had been apart for so many years since then. His father's death was in his memory only, and not in his emotions. Feelings which had seared and hurt once had cooled and hardened. He became sad at the thought of the change that comes over people in the course of their lives. He would have liked to stand beside his mother's grave today, with his mind full of kind thoughts about her, though those thoughts would cool in exactly the same way as his less kindly thoughts. But after the reading of the will, he felt that every sad thought he'd had during the week had been utterly futile.

And yet, as he listened to the happy shouts of his own children, along with those of his nieces and nephews, while he opened the gateway to his home, he felt the same lump coming to his throat that he had felt standing at his mother's grave.

13

Sioned showed no emotion when the news about the money was broken to her, and neither did she show any sign that she was about to give any of it to her family. She was exactly the same in the shop. The other girls would never have been able to tell that she had come into an inheritance. She went on with her work even more independently than before, if that were possible. The only one she showed any kind of pride to was Bertie Ellis, her latest boyfriend. The first night she went straight to him to tell him the news, and it was to him that she showed her true jubilation.

'And now,' she said, 'there's nothing to stop us getting married.'

'No, I don't suppose there is.'

'You don't suppose...?'

'Well, I don't know, I was just thinking –'

'Thinking what?'

'Thinking whether we could live on a guinea a week.'

'You're not going to be earning just a guinea a week forever. You'll get a pay rise eventually, I should hope.'

'Well, perhaps; I doubt it though. Trade is so slack at the moment, you see.'

'Oh well, we'll manage somehow; we can buy furniture with this money.'

'I don't like to take your money. If only I could win the anagram competition...'

'You'll never win on those competitions. It would be much better if you kept your sixpences.'

'You don't think much of my brains, then?'

'Not when it comes to solving puzzles, no.'

When the six hundred pounds that Sioned inherited from her grandmother was ready to be transferred to her, her parents had a talk with her about it one weekend. They both hated such conversations about money with their children, but with Sioned most of all. When a snail extends her horns out of her shell there's a chance of doing something with her, but when she insists on staying rolled up tight inside her shell....

'So, Sioned,' said her father, 'what are you going to do with that money, apart from putting it in the bank?'

The wind was taken out of her sails for a moment. She'd been left alone with her own counsel for so long in recent days that she had thought that no one was going to challenge her about the money.

'I don't know,' she said, twisting her pocket handkerchief around her fingers.

'Don't you think you'd like to give some of it to help the boys finish their Schooling?'

Sioned said nothing.

'And, in a way, the money belongs to your father,' said her mother.

'How's that?' she said, in a voice that suggested she

was afraid that her good luck was running out.

'Well,' said her father, 'it's not easy to explain, except that Mam saved that money while I was at home before I got married. There would be more, of course, if it weren't for the fact that Mam had to use some of it to live on.'

'The will says that the money belongs to me, though, doesn't it?'

'Yes, but we thought that you'd like to help your mother and father out a bit.'

'Why can't the boys help, the same way that you did?'

'That's neither here nor there, you know that very well. The boys have won their scholarships, so it's right for them to get a bit of education.'

'Well, I don't want to pay for their education. I want to get married.'

Neither of the two was surprised to hear this because they had steeled themselves to expect some thunderbolt or other from their daughter Sioned, who was so different from the rest of the children. The two became too sorrowful to be able to say anything.

When she came to herself, the mother said,

'So who is the young man, if it's not too much to ask?'

'A lad from the town.'

'What work does he do?'

'He's a clerk.'

'Who with?'

'Davies and Johnson.'

'Is he earning a decent wage?'

'Really I can't say.'

'Oh,' said the father, 'so you'd prefer to give this six hundred pounds to a stranger than to your own family.'

'I won't be giving him the money.'

'You be careful, my girl, or it won't be you who owns that money. It's a very odd thing that you should get married now, as soon as you get your hands on the money.'

Meanwhile in the cowshed, sitting on their pocket handkerchiefs spread out on the cow's manger, Owen and Twm were discussing the situation. Owen had finished his studies in the County School, but he didn't yet know the results of his exams, so the question of whether he would be going to College was still uncertain. But he knew that he would. His father and mother were sure to get hold of the money somehow, but that was the question – how to get it. A lot of money was needed to live in town for three years. Twm had only just started on his secondary education, and he wasn't really old enough to realize the economic pressures of living from day to day, but he was old enough to know that a substantial sum of money was needed to stay at School and that his father earned only a small salary.

'Just think,' said Owen, 'that it was Sioned who got that money; if only Elin or William or you or I had got it. But Sioned!'

'Yes,' said Twm, 'the money'll go like a hot knife through butter. She'll be swanking around the place with it.'

'Swanking?'*

'Yes, you know, cutting a dash.'

'Or she'll marry that bloke you saw her with.'

At this point, Bet came in; she picked up the milking stool from the gully and placed it directly in front of her brothers, then she sat down and stared at them. It was one of Bet's peculiar habits to do this with people she didn't see very often – she would stare at them as if amazed that there were such people in the world.

'Sioned is going to get married,' was her first piece of

114

news.

'Come off it; you've been eavesdropping on us from the hayshed, haven't you?'

'No – I've been listening in the house.'

Bet had gone into the house and caught the tail-end of the conversation between Sioned and her parents.

'She was telling Mam and Dad just now,' said Bet.

'Well, "farewell to you, Wales,"* said Twm, 'we'll never see a halfpenny of that money again.'

William appeared from somewhere.

'Hey, Will, have you heard the news?' said Twm loudly. 'Your sister Sioned is going to marry some Caernarfon lowlife.'

'Yes I know,' said he curtly, 'she'd rather share her money with strangers than with us.'

'What would you have done if you'd got the money?' asked Owen.

'I'd start up my own quarrying business.'

'And you'd share the money with the workers, like a true Socialist,' ventured Owen.

Hurt, William left them to it. His only hope these days was to escape from the claws of the Steward.

'So,' said Owen to Bet, 'how much of a chance have you got of winning a scholarship?'

'None at all,' she said, 'I can't do sums.'

Owen felt relieved to hear it. To have yet another member of the family winning a scholarship would be tempting Fate too much.

There was much heartache in Ffridd Felen on account of Sioned's decision to get married. Sometimes Jane Gruffydd felt like just telling her to go and never come back. But if she did that there'd be no end of talk in the district, and some of her in-laws, despite their hatred of Sioned, would be sure to make things even worse than before. The only consolation the mother had was that it all proved to those in Ifan's family who were against him that it wasn't the family of Ffridd Felen who were enjoying the spoils of Sioned Gruffydd's will after all. Some of them came there to commiserate. Their condolences were accepted for what they were worth, and the family members left again, scratching their heads and wondering how Jane Gruffydd could put up with everything so calmly.

On one matter only did Ifan and Jane Gruffydd put their foot down and that was that the wedding would not take place in Moel Arian.

Throughout the summer holidays this pain hovered above Ffridd Felen, and since Owen and Twm were at home all the time, they felt it most. Owen came close to going to look for work during the holidays, and had work been easy to come by he would have taken it. He and Twm ate as much as four people. They wore through their trousers and boots in no time at all. They helped as much as they could, carrying water, turning the handle of the butter churn, gathering heather to put off breaking into the hayrick, mucking out the cowshed and the pigsty, but there was still plenty of spare time left over and ample time for their mother to fret.

Sioned got married in town, dressed in a grey suit with yards of white tulle around her neck, while Bertie wore a silk hat and tails. Owen and Elin were there to represent the Ffridd Felen family, and both of them thanked God that the wedding was in town – just think of Bertie and his silk hat in Moel Arian! The more Owen saw of him, the more he thought of Twm's description of him

– a 'hobbledehoy.' He was one of those men who never grew up mentally and who continued to look eternally young. The two of them had to admit that Sioned looked very beautiful.

So it was that Sioned attained her dream of going to live in town, in a house with a parlour and a wooden floor – not a front room with a tiled floor like the one in Ffridd Felen; she had Venetian blinds, a plush sofa and cushions instead of a horsehair one with antimacassars.

Within a fortnight or so Sioned and Bertie came up from town on a Sunday afternoon. They had tea in the front room, and the best tea service was out. Everyone behaved unnaturally and was unhappy; the men ready too soon, and pacing around as people do before an important event like a prayer meeting or a funeral. Bet ran around in her new boots, which were high-buttoned and broad-toed, the stiff frills of her white apron protruding at the shoulders over a black and white dress that she'd inherited from her grandmother. Her hair, which had been plaited in dozens of little braids the night before, stuck out like a crinoline, and a lock of it was tied above the ear with a white ribbon. She followed the boys everywhere, clapping her hands rhythmically in front of her and behind her back. Jane Gruffydd was the most natural of them, since she was busiest, finishing off sprinkling sugar on the cake and dusting the teacups.

When the click of the gate was heard everyone except Bet felt uncomfortable. She ran to meet them and in her usual fashion she stared at them admiringly, and for her, a ten-year-old child, there really was something to admire: the white tulle fluttering around Sioned's face, and Bertie in his silk hat and tails. Owen's heart sank; he saw the

117

bride and groom walking up the aisle of the chapel and themselves, all the siblings, forming a retinue behind them, the eyes of everybody in the chapel piercing through their clothes and flesh to the very bone.

The tea was got through without much talking or eating. Everyone tried their best. The only one who didn't feel uncomfortable was Bet. She kept on asking for more apple cake until Twm gave her a kick under the table, and she looked at him with that innocent look which said that her sister's husband wasn't going to stop her eating anyway.

Once they thought that they'd found a general topic of conversation that they could talk about.

'You've got a very nice view from here,' said Bertie, who was sitting opposite the window.

'Yes,' said Ifan Gruffydd, 'it's rare to get such a wide view of mountain and sea.'

'You can see Ireland on a very clear day,' said Owen. But Bertie's store of remarks ran dry.

'Would you like a cigarette?' he asked his father-in-law.

'No, thanks, I prefer my pipe.'

'William?'

'No thanks.' He wanted one really, but he didn't want to show his brother-in-law that he wasn't used to smoking cigarettes.

As the time to go to chapel approached, Owen's heart sank further. He felt like putting his fingers down his throat to throw up, or do something else just for the excuse to stay at home.

And then the crucial question was asked by his father,

'What do you two want to do? Do you want to come to chapel?'

Sioned looked at Bertie and he at her.

'No, not this evening,' said he. 'We'll have to start our way back in a minute.'

Owen was so thankful that he felt like hugging him, but Ifan wasn't sure whether his son-in-law rose or fell in his estimation by refusing to come to chapel.

Owen and his mother stayed at home with the young couple, and they went around looking at the animals and other things. But Bertie really wasn't interested.

'Have you ever had a go at anagrams?' he asked Owen.

And for once Owen was forced to admit his ignorance to his brother-in-law.

'I don't know what anagrams are.'

'Like this,' said Bertie, pulling out a red book from his pocket. 'Here's a word, and you have to make two or three words to describe that word using the same letters that are in the word itself. With your brains you should be able to make up some good ones. I know a chap in town who won £300 for one.'

'Come on, now,' said Sioned, 'or we'll never get home.'

'Won't you have something to eat before you go?' said Jane Gruffydd.

'No, we'll go now, so that we can be out of the way before they get out of chapel,' said Sioned.

The afternoon showed Sioned that country people are not always that impressed by a grand appearance.

After they had gone, Owen said to his mother,

'Oh, give me something to eat – I'm starving!'

'Well, you should have eaten more at teatime. I don't know why a little nobody like that should have affected all your appetites in that way.'

14

Jane Gruffydd was in town about the middle of September the following year buying a trunk for Owen to take with him to College. He had won a £20 scholarship, and between that and the grant from the teacher training department Owen was able to get by at College apart from the cost of books and the College fees themselves. She walked around the shops slowly and without enthusiasm. It was one of those hot September days when the heat and haze of the day turns to a cold, clear moonlit night. People darted about in their summer clothes which were getting a new lease of life after weeks of wet weather in August. The shop windows and doorways were laden with ripe fruit, and wasps buzzed around them. The windows were filthy with the dirt of insects.

Jane Gruffydd had walked down to town in the midday sun, and her face was a ferment of sweat, her hair sopping as if she'd just been dragged out of the river. She had only one coat which she wore summer and winter. Despite this, she felt fairly contented. It was a weight off her mind that Owen had won the scholarship, and as Ann Ifans had said to her, she ought to be proud of her boy.

She went into the ironmonger's shop, which was cool after the hot street.

'These are in fashion now,' said the man, after she had told him what she wanted, pointing at some wooden boxes.

'How much is that?'

'Thirty shillings.'

Jane Gruffydd was taken aback.

'No, I'll have to have a cheaper one than that.'

'Well, here are some things which are popular at the moment,' and he showed her some big straw baskets with lids. She thought that it would do as long as he put his books in a sugar box.

Jane Gruffydd was glad that the basket cost less than she had expected. But shirts and other things cost more, and the pound that she'd kept from the month's wages disappeared like water through a sieve. She wondered whether she'd ever come to town and have more money in her pocket than she needed just for essentials. Yes, one day, she would. Owen would earn money one day; so would Twm. They would get good salaries; she would be able to pay off her debts and then be able to buy a few luxuries. In fact, she bought a few even now. She just had to take a few plums home with her.

After shopping she went to Sioned's house. Her daughter was glad to see her, and rushed to make her some tea. The redness of her face which was caused by the heat had given way to a yellowish pallor by this time, and Sioned could hardly fail to notice it.

'Are you feeling ill, Mam?'

'No, it's just that I rushed down to town in this heat.'

'It wasn't right that you had to walk. Why didn't you take the brake?'

'I'm going to take it on the way back, after popping in to see Elin for a minute. It's just too dear to take the brake both ways. Oh, this tea is good!'

'Are you feeling better now?'

'I'm back to my old self, don't worry.'

'You've got a big heavy coat on.'

'Yes, but it'll have to do; it'll be winter in no time.'

'Come and have a look around the house.'

And so the mother admired the plush chairs and the stained walnut furniture, and the latest fashion bed which was bristling with brass.

'I'll come with you as far as Nell's* place,' said Sioned, 'if you really have to go now.'

At Elin's place later Jane Gruffydd sat with her face turned to the window listening out for the brake which was about to arrive any minute. Elin's conversation always tended to make her forget about the time.

'Didn't Sioned offer you anything?'

'No, but she was very nice, and I had a good cup of tea from her.'

'Well, I should think that's the least she could do.'

'Well, I've certainly had less than that from Sioned; it's good to see that she's stopped sulking, and that she's capable of talking to you just like any other human being.'

'Huh! she could easily give you some of that six hundred pounds now that you've got such a lot to pay for.'

'I'd rather she didn't.'

And then came the sound of the horses' hooves that both of them knew so well, and the sound of the braking and the screeching of the wheels.

Elin waved to her mother, biting her lip to stop herself crying. Years of domestic service in the town had still not weaned her away from Ffridd Felen.

Owen's basket was tied to the side of the brake, swaying from side to side as the vehicle went on its way. To Jane Gruffydd the basket was a symbol of the beginning of the real tearing apart of her family. Although Elin and Sioned were now in the town, and the boys at School, she didn't feel that they had left home because they were still so close. She couldn't take her eyes off the basket, which seemed to her like some malevolent Fate. In the middle of the week like this the brake was full of women, and they were much keener to talk than if the company had been mixed.

'When is Owen going to be starting in the College?' said one.

'In three weeks' time.'

'You'll be very sad to see him go.'

'I will be for a while, I'm sure.'

'But that's the way it is, once they start leaving home.'

'Yes, and there's nothing much around here to keep the boys at home.'

'No, there isn't, and it's even worse for the grown-ups. But your boys will end up in much better places.'

'I don't know; anything can happen. There's plenty of expense to drive them on to make a go of it, anyway.'

By this time a breeze had got up, and the haze over the sea had lifted. The corn stood in stooks all over the fields; some was being harvested on carts. The sea was right beside them now, and it looked different from the way it looked from the perspective of Ffridd Felen. There were dark shadows upon it, and its colour was deeper. Jane Gruffydd turned her head to see Moel Arian, and it, too, looked different, with its windows blinking at her as the sun's rays fell on them. The stillness of September was upon the countryside, and there was just a hint of a change of colour in the trees. Jane Gruffydd's spirit became calm and accepting under the influence of the landscape, while the horses pulled them slowly up the steep hill, their hooves resounding on the hard ground of the road and steam rising from their bodies. The next generation, who would come to take this journey by car, would not experience this calming of the spirit, nor would they see such views over the tops of the hedges.

Everyone still at home in Ffridd Felen regressed to being small children when their mother went to town, and they rushed excitedly for her basket before she even had time to take off her coat.

She didn't have to do any housework when she got back. The boys had dug some potatoes for a 'quarry supper', and they had already milked the cows, two hours earlier than usual so that their mother could have a rest when she reached the house.

'My dear little ones,' she said, 'their poor udders will be almost bursting tomorrow morning, and I'll have to get up at the crack of dawn to milk them.'*

15

Early on a Monday morning in December 1908 the kitchen in Ffridd Felen was as busy, if not busier, than if it were midday. It was only four o'clock, yet William and his father and mother were at the table eating their breakfast. Twm and Bet were sitting by the fire under the big chimney breast, drinking a cup of tea on the hob, and they would have been perfectly happy if it weren't for the fact that they knew why they were there. Usually, nothing gave Bet greater pleasure than to get up at some unearthly hour, to slip her dress on over her nightie, and to have breakfast by the fire. Although it was only four o'clock there was a blazing fire in the grate and the kitchen was warm. Jane Gruffydd had been on her feet since half past two, though William's pack had been ready since the night before. In Ffridd Felen no matter how early anyone – except Jane herself – got up, they never went into a kitchen with the cold chill of a just-lit fire.

William was going to the South, and he would be catching the mail coach at Bron Llech station.

'Remember to hold your clothes in front of the fire before putting them on, now, William. They're well aired now, but you'd better show them to the fire when you get there. And watch out that you don't sleep in a damp bed. I hope you'll get decent lodgings with someone from around here.'

'There are plenty of people from around these parts down there, so they say, but Jack says I'd be better off staying with some Southerners,* that it'd be better in the long run.'

'Very likely,' said his father, 'those Southerners won't be writing to anybody around here.'

'And remember to write to say that you've arrived safely. Have you got that postcard in your pocket now?'

'Yes.'

By this time William was sitting in the armchair with his foot up on the fender tying his shoelace, putting his head down as low as possible so that no one could see that he was on the verge of bursting into tears. This was the first time he had ever been away from home, even for one night.

'And I hope you'll get some good company on the journey,' said his mother, 'and that you won't catch cold.'

The mother kept talking for the same reason that William was keeping his head down.

With that, William gets his coat and his hard hat on, and wraps a long scarf twice around his neck; then he grabs the basket that's been lying in wait on the big table since yesterday evening like Fate itself, the same basket that had danced at the side of the brake four years before, the one that Owen had used to go away to College. When William went to the South, it was Owen who got the new bag.

'Well,' said William, 'goodbye to you all'; and without looking at anyone he followed his father out into the darkness. His mother went to get the lamp to light them on their way, but a gust of wind came and sent a tongue of flame up the glass before extinguishing it altogether. She

126

ran to get the lamp off the table, but by the time she got back out, all she could see were two shadows by the gate, and one of them calling 'Have you found it?' as he groped around. Then they were wrapped in darkness, and they disappeared amid whispers. She shut the door and went to sit by the fire, where Twm and Bet were still staring dreamily into the flames. And a heavy stillness descended upon the kitchen which a minute before had been full of talk and the stomping of feet.

'Well,' said Jane Gruffydd, 'there's no use me dozing off here. Get to bed, Bet, and you, Twm. It's too long for you to stay up until it's time to go to School.'

She set to clearing the kitchen and cleaning boots.

This was the morning she had been dreading for weeks. Ever since William had said defiantly that he could no longer put up with being a beggar in the quarry and that he'd made up his mind to go to the South, she had felt as if there was a weight lying on her heart. All the other children were fairly close by, but the South – was at the ends of the earth! And it had been taken for granted somehow that William would never leave home except to get married. But here he was going to somewhere at the back of beyond, and to do a completely different kind of job. Life was very hard. But really, she didn't know which was worse, seeing William leaving home, or seeing him come home every night down in the mouth and depressed. Ifan said that he'd go too if he were younger. Wages in the valley had reached their lowest point ever.

Ifan Gruffydd was soon home again, having walked back with the postman. He would now have to start on his three-mile journey to work, and today, for the first time, he'd be alone.

127

In the train, William sat with his head resting on his hand, and his sadness lying like a lump in his chest. The train went past houses with little, round, feeble lights shining out from their windows. He could imagine the wife cutting bread and butter, filling the food-tin, and pouring tea into the flask. He saw the husband taking the dirty handkerchief out of his pocket and discarding it, taking a clean one from the drawer, and there, warming on the fender, were his boots, still black today, a Monday morning, having been greased, and the grease still wet in the holes of the laces, sweating in the heat of the fire. Then the husband putting his head around the door, and calling into the house, 'No, it's not raining, I won't take a sack today.' Then throwing an old coat over his shoulders and closing it with a safety pin, turning the pin towards his shoulder.

'Oh God,' groaned William, 'why couldn't it be me starting out for work like that?'

And yet, he remembered his recent hatred of the quarry. He could see it now in his mind's eye, lying black over there on the side of the mountain, the mist like a grey cap on its head, like some old witch making fun of him, as he groped towards her on dark mornings like this one, and to have no work to start on in the chill of the morning; just having to go around with his hands in his pockets, begging. That's all it was, there was no getting away from it. Going from one table to the next, and standing there mutely. A few of the men would give him a block of slate, but more often than not he would be refused; the refusal was sometimes given cordially on account of a real shortage of good blocks, but other refusals were cold, and still others were falsely apologetic to cover up sheer niggardliness. There was nothing better than being a 'rubbler'* to get to know men's true natures.

There was old --------------- (William simmered with rage as he recalled him now) who had cunningly refused to give him a block one afternoon that summer. That afternoon, just before the hooter went for the end of the shift, a load of rocks came out of the pit to -------------, and he decided to ask him for some rocks the first thing the following morning. In his bed that night something plagued him, and he went to work half an hour earlier than usual. As he had expected, who was there hard at it but -------------, who had sawn a large number of blocks already and had built up a big heap of split slates on his bench. He felt such loathing for the man then that he couldn't bring himself to ask for a block, but he made sure that everyone in the quarry knew about what had happened.

And at the end of the month, it was so hard to bear the scowls of the slate marker if he didn't have enough slates, and then he would literally have to go and beg for some blocks.

Then he thought of his father, who had to work according to set terms, often unfavourable ones, so that he had no idea if he would be paid for his labour at the end of the month. The quarryman's wages were like a lucky dip.*
And then there had been all the small strikes that had happened in recent years. Five weeks here and two months there. Not a halfpenny coming in from anywhere during those periods, and everybody eating more rations than usual because of sitting around at home doing nothing. His mother was heroic in the way she was able to face up to the shopkeeper, and the shopkeeper himself had to be patient.

And the quarrymen were blind, in his view, not to see that they needed to join the Union, and to fight for a minimum wage and a set standard for wage negotiations.

A few more had joined recently, but not half enough. What use was it for them to make a fuss and come out on strike if they didn't have the strength of the Union to back them up? Well, it was up to them if they preferred to lick the chains that kept them in slavery!

William's thoughts ran on in this way, as the train moved slowly on, puffing like a man climbing a steep hill. It stopped in a depressing-looking little station which was as silent as the grave except for the sound of the steam hissing from the train. In the midst of the darkness a porter held aloft a lantern, which shed its beams out in a circle in the morning mist. He turned it once more and the train moved on at a slow pace out of the station, and the porter and his lamp were buried in its darkness. William tired of turning things over in his mind, and he fell asleep.

Later on the journey the quarry again forced itself vividly into his mind. He was drawing towards the end of his journey; it was getting dark once more. William forgot about his fellow-travellers. All he could see were the lads in the shed, their caps drawn down low on their heads, and a hungry, grey look about them, shivering in the cold as they stood in the doorway waiting for the hooter. Every now and again, they stuck their heads around the doorpost, like rats peeping out from their holes. Then, as soon as the hooter went, they headed off like a pack of bloodhounds down the metalled road towards the mountain. He remembered those faces now, rough on the surface but concealing much tenderness. They were capable of laughing when things were at their bleakest, and could find something funny even in a poor wage. So many of them died of tuberculosis.

He started to boil with rage again as he thought about the quarry. He would have liked to kill Morris Ifan, the

130

Little Steward. He knew that Morris had something personal against his father, and that he would like to get rid of Ifan, but his father was able to keep his temper, something that William just couldn't do. Now he was reliving the scene on the day when he got the sack. He had gone to Buckley the Chief Steward to ask for something better than 'rubbling,'* but he had not been there, and so William had been forced to convey his message to Morris Ifan. He remembered his scorn. That was bad enough but when he started to reproach him for his connections with the Labour Party and his Union work William could stand it no longer, and he fell upon him and grabbed him by the neck. It was lucky for the Little Steward that someone had come by just then. His hatred for the man still made his blood boil, and he started to feel more optimistic about going to work in the coal mine.

16

The day that William went away was a strange day in Ffridd Felen. The mother's heart wasn't in doing the usual Monday washing, nor in doing anything else, so she went up to Twnt i'r Mynydd in the afternoon.

'I was thinking of you,' said Ann Ifans, 'I was going to pop by this evening. I would have come down this morning but there's something wrong with this old cow here.'

'Oh no, really?'

'It's nothing much. She drank too much water when she went out for a bit yesterday, and she came in again trembling all over.'

'But isn't there some new trouble all the time? It's as if these bad times weren't enough to put up with for any poor creature....'

'Quite right. It's a terrible world.'

'I don't remember such a terrible time, although Mam says it was worse when she was young.'

'That's what my mother says too. But you don't expect it to carry on being so bad all the time; you expect things to get better.'

'But they don't, do they?' said Ann Ifans, with that note of doom in her voice that's characteristic of cheerful people. 'But how was William before he went?'

'I think he was almost overcome but that he was trying to hold it together.'

'His father will miss him in the quarry.'

'Oh, yes, terribly.'

'But you'll see, William will be fine once he gets there and starts earning some money. They tell me there's very good wages to be had down in the South there.'

'I hope so, indeed, but so many get killed in those coal mines.'

'As far as that goes, there's plenty of men getting killed in these quarries, and countless people dying of TB.'

'That's true enough.'

'And as for those shops in town ... I wouldn't put my dog to work there, let alone a child.'

'Yes, you're right, and their wages are so low.'

'A pittance, yes; think of John here, getting only fifteen shillings a week after working for years on end for nothing, standing behind the counter all day from the crack of dawn, and that old man pacing around the shop, keeping an eagle eye on everything. If it was possible for him to buy more eyes to stick in his head, he'd do it, so he could keep a better watch that nobody was stealing anything.'

Jane Gruffydd laughed.

'How's Owen?'

'He's well; I got a letter from him this morning – he likes his new place just fine.'

'It's good that somebody's happy.'

'But mind you, his wages are nowhere near what they should be, considering the cost of his education.'

'No, I'm sure they aren't.'

'He pays ten shillings a week for his lodgings and has to buy his own food.'

'God save the poor thing!'

'Yes, and the poor creature tries to send a bit home to us every month.'

'Fair play to him. Owen's a good little lad.'

'Yes,' said Jane Gruffydd. 'But not one of them has given me such pain as Sioned has, you know.'

'How is she and her husband, and the little boy?'

'Oh, they're fine. The baby's a dear little thing, but I can't do anything with that husband of hers. I don't think he's got a particle of sense in him. But you won't get anything out of Sioned – she keeps it all hidden away in her carpet bag. It would have been much fairer for us or Geini to get Ifan's mother's money.'

'She didn't give you any of it?'

'Not a halfpenny. It would come in so useful now! And there's Twm, too, who'll be off to College before long.'

And so the two women talked about their lives, without understanding any of the causes of their situation. But they were fully alive to the effects. They had no choice but to go on from day to day, hoping that things would improve. But being able to chat with a neighbour was in itself a load off your mind.

Ifan Gruffydd was a full ten minutes later than usual reaching home that evening. He went to sleep in the armchair as soon as he had eaten his supper. His wife noticed the dark bags under his eyes and his calloused hands. The long December evening seemed interminable to her. But the next day she would get a postcard from William.

One thing that changes once children leave home is

134

the sudden importance that the postman begins to acquire. When a family is all together at home, to receive a letter is an historic event. But once the children begin to leave, receiving letters becomes more and more common and the postman is a prominent figure in your life.

However, though she waited and waited as she stood at the washing-up bowl the following day, not a word came. In Jane Gruffydd's imagination, the South was three times further away than it was in reality. Despite that, she expected to get a letter in half the time that it actually took to arrive from there.

The card arrived on the Wednesday morning, and when William mentioned on it that he had had company on his journey, his mother felt that the journey had taken place at least a month ago.

Within a few days, a letter came from him, a short letter full of clipped sentences which expressed nothing of his true feelings. He said that he had got work and lodgings with some very kind Southerners. There was not a word about his homesickness, nor his shyness as he had to wash in a tub in front of the fire, nor about the dark-eyed girl in the house where he lodged. The nearest he approached to expressing his longing was in a postscript where he said that the loaf of bread and the butter that his mother had put in his basket had been very good.

It was down to Twm to write a letter back that Sunday. Twm was a peerless letter-writer, except that his letters conveyed the atmosphere of home so vividly that they made the recipient's homesickness even worse.

17

At this time, Twm was in his final two years in the County School, and because he had to concentrate so hard on his work he was once again lodging in the town. At first he went to stay with Sioned, his sister. She seemed keen to have him, although his parents felt that they would rather he went to stay with a stranger. He took most of his food down with him. He bought the ingredients for his dinner in town, and he paid his sister three shillings a week. Before long his butter, his bread, his bacon and his eggs began to run out before the end of the week. He knew that that shouldn't be happening, since he could count how many eggs he was eating, even if he couldn't keep tabs on the other food.

One week his bread, eggs and bacon had run out by Thursday morning, and he had to buy a loaf of bread with his pocket money. This had happened once before, but he had had more money then. This time, though, he couldn't afford to buy anything apart from the loaf. On Friday morning at breakfast Sioned said,

'You've eaten a lot this week.' Offering him a pat of some soft, shop-bought butter, she said,

'Here, you can have some of my butter.'

Twm lost his temper.

'Your butter indeed; keep your rubbish! It wasn't me who ate the pound of butter I brought from home on Monday morning, and it wasn't me who ate the eggs either. I've only had four of them.'

Sioned slumped in her chair and started to cry, and Bertie glared at Twm as if he had just murdered his sister.

'You should be ashamed of yourself, upsetting Janet* like that. Are you accusing your sister of stealing your food?' he said, in that affected, effeminate voice of his.

'No, I'm not,' said Twm, raising himself to his full height, which was pretty tall by this time, and towering over his brother-in-law. 'I know that she borrowed my food because she doesn't get enough from you.'

Sioned started bawling at this, and Eric the little boy came downstairs also in tears. Bertie attempted to stand on his dignity, saying to Twm, with his arm around his wife,

'You'd better leave this house right now.'

'I'm going,' said Twm. 'I was a fool to come here in the first place. I've seen things that I really didn't want to see.'

He grabbed his bag and went to School, with the sound of Sioned's crying still resounding in his ears. He called for his friend, Arthur, on his way. He was still having his breakfast of bacon and eggs.

'Hello,' he said, seeing Twm there so early and so white about the gills, 'what's up?'

'Nothing,' said Twm, giving his friend a wink behind his mother's back, 'I just got up early, and thought I'd take a stroll on the quay before going to School.'

When they got outside he was able to explain to

Arthur what had happened.

'Come back with me this very minute,' he said, 'so that you can have some breakfast.'

'No, I won't come now,' said Twm, 'I can't eat anything at the moment. But I'll come to have a bit of dinner with you later if I can.'

'Of course, you're welcome,' said Arthur, who was a shopkeeper's son and knew that there would be something for dinner every day.

'But nobody's to know about this except you and Elin. I'll have to make up some story, and I'll go to Elin's for my tea, and tell her all about it.'

'Mam,' said Arthur at lunchtime, 'can Tommy have some dinner with us? His sister's not very well and has had to go to bed.'

'Of course, with pleasure, my boy; what's the matter with your sister?'

'I don't know, but she's not very well.'

'Well, look, wouldn't it be better for you to stay here with Arthur until she gets better?'

'We'll see,' said Twm. 'I'll go up there from School this afternoon to see how she is.'

'Well, yes, you haven't got the time to look after yourself, with this year being such an important one for you at School.'

Instead of going to Sioned's house for tea, Twm went to Elin's and told her everything.

'Well,' said Elin, shaking her head, 'I said that no good would come of that marriage. But we have to hide this from Mam.'

'Well, I'm not going back there to stay, anyhow, even if Sioned and that little corgi of hers begged me to on their hands and knees.'

'Why?'

'Oh, I don't know, I just don't like that Bertie, and I don't like getting too close to a husband and wife who are only pretending to be a couple. I felt like hitting that Bertie this morning, seeing him holding Sioned so tenderly, and knowing that she probably isn't the only one he holds like that.'

'Twm!'

'Alright, maybe it's just me being suspicious. I'd better not say any more. But what shall we do now? – that's the question.'

'Look, go and stay with Arthur until Saturday, since they've been so kind, and go to the woman who keeps the old lodging house that you used to stay in to ask if you can go back there, and then you can tell Mam that you can't study properly in Sioned's house because Eric makes too much noise.'

Jane Gruffydd believed Twm's reason for changing his lodgings since it was a reasonable enough excuse. It didn't dawn on her that anything was wrong in her daughter's house. When she asked Twm on Saturday how Sioned was, he had his answer ready. He would say that he'd seen her the previous evening. But in reality he never saw her except sometimes in passing on the street. When he went there on the Monday after the row to pay for his lodging Sioned was as snooty as Bertie, and she didn't ask him to call again.

18

It was almost Christmas, a time of year that changes its meaning for parents as their children grow up. When the children were small Christmas was a busy, happy time in Ffridd Felen; busy because everyone was practising for the Literary Festival that lasted two days; happy because the children did not expect to get any presents, except for the prizes they might win in the Literary Festival. Ann and Bob Ifans, Twnt i'r Mynydd, came there on Christmas Eve, and the children all went together to the Festival. Ann Ifans brought some of her home-made toffee to Ffridd Felen, and she had some of Ffridd Felen's home-made toffee to take home with her. The smallest children always enjoyed the toffee-making. After they had gone to bed their mother brought them some fresh toffee and popped it in their mouths, warning them not to take it out again in case they got it stuck in the bedclothes. If the mouthful of toffee was a big one it was quite hard work to turn it around and around in their mouths. Their jawbones would start to ache.

But by 1908 things had changed. The eldest children

were away, and Twm and Bet were too old for Christmas to be really exciting for them. Owen would come home, and perhaps Elin would come up on Christmas afternoon. Sioned and her husband and the baby might come, but Jane didn't really care either way about them.

A few days before Christmas she went down to town and called with Elin on her way.

'I don't know whether I ought to ask Sioned and her husband to come up at Christmas,' she said.

'I don't think she'd come, you know,' said Elin, remembering why Twm had left.

'Do you think?'

'No, she won't; I heard her say something about staying at home, that she was having some kind of tea party or something.'

'Oh. How is she getting on, do you know?'

'Alright, as far as I know.'

The welcome Jane Gruffydd received in Sioned's house was not as warm as the last time. Sioned was busy making pies.

'I'll make you a cup of tea as soon as I've put these in the oven,' she said in a tone of voice which indicated that she would rather not make the tea.

'There's no need for you to go to any trouble,' said her mother. 'I've promised to go to Elin's.'

Sioned cheered up on hearing this.

'Wait two minutes, then. I'll come and sit down with you now.'

While Sioned was in the back kitchen with her pies, her mother looked around the front room. It wasn't quite the same as it had been the last time. Everything looked rather shabby and dismal, and Eric himself was quite grubby, playing with a dirty old wooden horse. You couldn't say that the room was dirty, exactly, but it wasn't clean either.

Before long Sioned came in, wearing a kind of oilcloth apron with a tear in it.

'I'm making a few mince pies* now,' she said. 'I've already made my cake.'

'Cake? Is there some special cake apart from *bara brith** for Christmas then?' said her mother, annoyed.

'Yes, I mean *bara brith*.'

'Well, say what you mean, then.'

Sioned paid no attention to the rebuke. She went on, 'Bertie's bringing a goose home tonight – a present from a friend of his.'

'That's lucky for you, though I wouldn't particularly want one.'

'We're going to have lots of friends over to tea on Christmas Day and Boxing Day.'

'You won't be able to come home to us, then?'

'No. Had someone said that we were coming?'

'No, nobody,' curtly.

'I thought perhaps Nell* had said something to you, because she thinks that we all do the same as she does.'

'Elin never said a word to me,' said Jane Gruffydd, riled.

'We'd like to come, but these friends of Bertie's are coming over. They're very nice people.'

'I'm sure,' said her mother. 'I'm off now then. Come here, darling,' she said to Eric, who was sitting underneath the sewing machine, 'here's a bit of toffee for you.'

Eric ran to get the toffee, and grabbed it from his grandmother's hand.

'Say "thank you",'* said his mother.

Eric looked into the paper bag.

'Now then, Eric, say "thank you" to grandma for the toffee ... Eric, say "thank you".'

There was a piece of toffee in Eric's mouth.

'Leave him alone,' said his grandmother.

Jane Gruffydd had a pound of butter in her basket which she had been intending to give Sioned, but she took it home with her instead.

She was in a bit of a temper by the time she reached Elin's place.

'I don't know why I go there.'

'Go where?' asked Elin.

'To see Sioned.'

'What was the matter with her today?'

'I don't know. She was on her high horse for some reason. She obviously didn't want to see me, anyhow.'

'Didn't she offer you a cup of tea?'

'Yes, but only in an offhand way. Anyhow, I said I was on my way to see you.'

'You did the right thing.'

'The little minx, with her mince pies and her cake and her goose.'

'Is she going to have a goose?' Elin stood stock still, in the middle of cutting a slice of bread.

'Yes. Bertie's getting one as a present according to her.'

'Yes, I'm sure.'

'And some of his friends are going there for tea at Christmas, says she. Some very nice people.'

'Yes, they're all nice in Sioned's eyes if they speak English and wear bracelets.'*

'Tell me, can they live like that and pay their way?'

'Yes, as far as I know. He got a pay rise recently.'

'I thought everything looked a bit dingy, and that little

boy was quite grubby.'

'Yes, he is. She takes no pride in looking after him.'

There was a pained look on Jane Gruffydd's face as she walked to catch the brake.

'I'll be up at Christmas.'

'Yes, come soon.'

Her mother pulled her fur stole tight around her neck. She was wearing the same coat as she had worn six years before in the prize-giving ceremony, and the same hat, too, but remodelled.

19

After dinner on Christmas Day, Owen and Twm sat in the kitchen in Ffridd Felen putting the world to rights instead of going to the Literary Festival as they used to do when they were children. Indoors everything was comfortable, a bright fire in the grate making Y Fawnog's furniture shine. (Owen had managed to persuade his father to buy the furniture after old Sioned Gruffydd's death and share the payment among his siblings.) Outside everywhere was grey and comfortless. They had just had a good dinner of beef, baked potatoes and pudding with a butter sauce. That morning the postman had brought a letter containing a postal order for ten shillings from William and a Christmas card in English from Sioned. Elin came up in person in the afternoon.

A whole term had gone by since Owen and Twm had had a chance to talk, and Owen was eager to pump Twm for information about Sioned, since he had noticed his mother's pained look as she flung Sioned's card unceremoniously on the dresser. So this afternoon Owen heard the story of Twm's falling out with Sioned, a story that Twm had not liked to tell in a letter.

'Those two will come a cropper one day,' said Owen.

'Let them get on with it,' said Twm. 'Everyone worries far too much about them. They've chosen to live like that, and everyone seems to have forgotten by now how badly she behaved over that money.'

'Yes,' said Owen, thinking and pondering what a strange thing family was. Portraits of some of the family were looking down on him now from the walls of the room. Sometimes he felt like smashing them up so that he could forget his family history. And yet, it was impossible to cut himself off from them, as impossible as it was to cut himself off from the pain caused him by some of them who were still alive. There they were, falling out and making up, then falling out all over again; he hated them so much that he felt he could kill them. Many times while he was at College Owen had felt that he could have killed Sioned for playing such a dirty trick, since he was living from hand to mouth without the bare necessities. But then, when he saw her, he would talk to her without showing any of that hatred. Why couldn't they leave their family alone?

'There's no point in worrying,' said Twm, seeing him staring pensively into the fire.

'I wouldn't worry about it myself, but I know that it worries Mam. Does she know why you left?'

'No, but I think she suspects that there's something not quite right there. She went down there this week and didn't get much of a welcome from Sioned.'

'The little bitch!'

'Sioned was a little madam showing off about her

mince pies and her goose.'

'Can they afford things like that?'

'No they can't, that's for sure. They can't unless Bertie won on the horses, that is. He's given up on the anagrams.'

Owen laughed.

'I bet the money's all gone by now,' he said.

'Quite likely, and she'll be up here like a shot when she hasn't got a penny.'

'No, she won't,' Owen said hotly, 'I'll see to it that she won't.'

'Yes, but it won't be you who makes that decision, my lad. What should have been done at the time of the fuss about Gran's will, after we found out what Sioned was going to do with the money, was she should have been told to keep away for ever, and have been cut completely out of the family.'

'Perhaps you're right.'

'But why are we worrying about these things before they happen? We worry far too much about the family as it is instead of leaving them alone. I gave up fretting about Sioned long ago.'

'Yes, but you can't somehow.'

'Some people can. Sioned couldn't care less how much pain she causes others, and why should we have to do our duty all the time when she doesn't?'

'It would be pretty awful for Dad and Mam if we were all like Sioned.'

'But the rest of us can do too much because one of us does nothing.'

Owen felt that there was a lot of truth in what Twm was saying.

The two went for a stroll along the lane before tea.

The district was like a perfect picture of the greyness of winter: bare trees, russet fields, grey sea, grey mist, and everything soaking wet underfoot.

'Do you like being home at this time of the year?' Twm asked.

'I like being in the house,' said Owen, 'but look at this place, what a picture of hopelessness. Whoever thought it was a good idea to build a house in a place like this?'

'The person who did that was escaping from poverty, don't you see? A man will do anything to survive. And, look, we've been trying to escape from poverty here ever since.'

'I never thought of it like that,' said Owen.

'How did you think we first came here, then?'

'I suppose I just assumed that we'd always been here.'

'Ask Auntie Geini to tell you her grandmother's story, and my father's grandmother for that matter, our great-grandmother; we started out from over there,' said Twm, pointing at Yr Eifl,* 'the same place that Mam came from years after.'

'Guess what,' said Twm to Owen later on, 'I've entered an *englyn** in the poetry competition at the festival tonight.'

Owen looked at him admiringly. He was a tall, strapping, handsome lad.

They went to the Literary Festival that night, each having a special interest in being there. The chapel was full and it was warm inside, the lamps burning brightly and everyone looking happy. Everything there was the same as it had been ten years before – the same strip of calico draped across the front of the stage with 'Moel Arian Literary and Music Festival' written on it in big red and blue letters, the same smell of varnish on the seats, which children kicked underneath, the same smell of oranges, and the officials on the stage wearing the same kinds of ribbons.

Twm won the prize for the *englyn*, and from that point until the end of the evening the two of them enjoyed everything – the singing and the recitation (which was pretty poor if truth be told), the improvised speech (which was funny), the judging of the home-made cradles, socks and oat loaves (which was interesting), and the choirs which brought the festival to a jubilant close.

The holidays were coming to an end. The main pleasure of the break for Owen was the opportunity to be at home to laze about and talk. He had been a Latin teacher in Tre Ffrwd* since September. After spending three years in College, he had got a second class honours degree in Latin. The College hadn't made much of an impression on him. Perhaps that was his own fault as much as it was the College's. He had made friends, he'd talked and debated with his fellow students, he'd spent hours musing over his work, and had to think constantly about the best way to survive on next to nothing. He didn't take part in sport at all because it cost money, and he closed his eyes to stop himself seeing the beautiful girls who filled the halls of residence. By this time he regretted neglecting so many aspects of College life. His degree wouldn't have been one iota worse for it. But at the time the lack of money forced him to keep his nose firmly in his books. Once he had got a place there, he wanted to keep it, and the only way of doing so was to work, or so he thought then. He had had to sacrifice a lot of pleasures, but that helped him to save money.

He always remembered his father's small wage packet, and the shop bills piling up, and from his ten pounds a month salary he always tried to send about three pounds home. The single teachers at the School used to enjoy themselves. They would go to Liverpool on Saturdays, they'd buy tickets to go to plays and concerts. When there was nothing else to do, they would play cards in each other's digs. The married ones had to save. They wore suits that had seen better days to School, keeping the good suits for Sundays. They aimed to give their children an education, and to buy books. The School routine became familiar to them. They ceased to make an effort, they never gave new lessons, they worked out their own system of marking work without bothering to read it, and they laughed at a youngster like Owen who diligently prepared his lessons and who carried exercise books home to mark them.

'You'll get tired of doing that,' they said.

'Perhaps,' said Owen. 'I expect you were like me at my age.'

He didn't want the headmaster to find fault with him in his first term at any rate.

At present he didn't have much of a chance to do anything other than work since he couldn't afford to enjoy himself like the other single teachers.

As the time approached for him to go back after the Christmas holidays, Owen wondered whether it would always be like this. In those days pay rises for teachers were a matter of luck and chance. His mother would finish paying off her bills one day. But perhaps Twm wouldn't win a scholarship to College. He had the ability, but he was so blasé about his work, and so blasé about his family too. He wondered whether Twm would shoulder the burden when he had finished College and got a job. He doubted it, and yet there was a lot of truth in what Twm had said on Christmas Day about family, that it was possible for some individuals to do too much. But there it was, you were born that way, he supposed; one person had a conscience and another didn't have one. Then it dawned on him that these things wouldn't be bothering him at all if everyone did their duty. It was the fact that Sioned didn't do hers that made him complain that he was doing his. If everyone pulled their weight, there was no reason for anyone to blame anyone else. There was a lot of sense in what Twm had said about throwing Sioned out of the family.

These were the things Owen was turning over and over in his mind as he prepared to go back to work. His mother was happier than she had been on Christmas Day. Gradually she was beginning to be able to pay off some of her debts in the shops.

20

On a Monday morning in June 1912, Jane Gruffydd had been busy with the washing from early on, thinking about this and that, especially the letters she'd received from the boys. Twm had gone to College in 1910 on a slightly more generous scholarship than Owen's, but since there was a rule that he couldn't join the teacher's training department in his first year without having been a pupil teacher beforehand, he was actually worse off.

Bet had gone into domestic service, so that Ifan and Jane were quite on their own by this time. Thirty-two years had gone by since their marriage, and they were conscious of getting old. Ifan looked tired out all the time, and he wasn't able to work so much on the smallholding when he got home at night. It took Jane much longer to get through the work of the day, and she often had to take a rest. She would have liked to keep Bet at home. Their hair was going grey. Their bodies were clumsier, and the colours of their eyes faded. To the emptiness of their lives there came stirrings of feeling they they had known nothing of when all the children had been at home. Life had gone on then uneventfully, without their giving a second thought to the postman, let alone waiting eagerly for him to come. Now letters came from the boys every week. Neither of them ever had any news, and saying as much helped to fill up the sheets of paper in some measure. It was Twm who wrote the longest letters, because he had a talent for writing and because there was more going on in a college than in a coal mine or a School, and his letter was often full of a list of the many expenses that he had at the college, and a little appeal at the end for a sub from his mother.

William came home from the South every summer. He looked smart in a navy blue suit (a sure sign for the people of Moel Arian that someone was living a respectable life and had not become one of the riff-raff) and he talked about the South as if it were next door to heaven. There were pretty good wages to be had there. Most of the colliers believed in the Union, and the Labour Party was growing strongly. He wore a white silk scarf around his neck which increased the pallor of his face. Yet, by the time he prepared to leave again at the end of the fortnight, he was talking less about the South, and he took to lying around in the fields and gazing out to sea.

This morning his mother was thinking mainly about Twm, since she was busy washing his clothes and she knew he was in the middle of his examinations. She wondered how he was getting on in sultry weather like this.

It was eleven o'clock, close and cloudy, and she was regretting not having Bet at home – if it were only to make her a cup of tea by the time she finished. She was weak with hunger, but she was too hot and exhausted to go and prepare something for herself. Then she heard the click of the latch on the gate, and she wasn't annoyed about the interruption today, as she was ready to loiter around with anyone by this time. She heard footsteps approach the cowshed, where she did the washing in the summer, and she was surprised to see Elin there. Just one look at her face told her that she was bringing bad news.

'What is it?' said her mother.

'Don't upset yourself, Mam. Come into the house.'

In the darkness of the kitchen they couldn't see a thing. Elin gave the fire a poke.

'It's Sioned. She's in trouble.'

'What is it?'

'Bertie's run off.'

'He's what?'

Jane sat down slowly in a chair, and Elin shook the kettle to see if there was any water in it. Then she put it on the fire and sat down herself.

'Yes, he's run away.'

Jane Gruffydd fell silent; she could think of nothing at all to say. But then,

'They were up here only last week,' she said, just as if Bertie had dropped dead rather than run off.

Elin said, 'He was at work on Saturday morning as usual, and he went to the station. From there he sent a boy with a message to Sioned saying that he'd been called away suddenly on business, and that he'd be back by Sunday evening without fail. But he didn't come back. On Saturday afternoon his boss went to check the accounts and he found that he was thirty pounds short, and he came up to tell Sioned this morning.'

'Did you see Sioned?'

'No; it was a neighbour of hers who came over to tell me, and I thought it best to come up here and tell you instead of going to see Sioned, in case you got to hear of it some other way, because the news will travel like a forest fire before long.'

'Yes, you're right,' said the mother, and she shut her eyes and gave a long sigh, then,

'We'll be disgraced, and so will the boys, even though they've had an education. How will I be able to hold my head up in this place any more?'

'It's no disgrace on anybody except on the man himself. Anyone with any sense knows that it's not your fault.'

'Perhaps, but there'll be plenty of people clapping their hands with joy that we're being taken down a peg or two.'

'Don't take any notice, we know what kind of people those are.'

Elin started to get the tea ready. She gave vent to the feelings that had been building up inside her on the way up by crashing about with the crockery.

'That sly little rascal,' she said. 'But never mind him, come and have a cup of tea, and a bite to eat, just as if nothing had happened.'

She tried to do that. She thought it would be so nice just to have that tea with Elin, with nothing to worry her.

'The worst thing,' said Elin, 'will be working out what to do with Sioned and the child, because they're bound to be left without a halfpenny.'

This was the first time that Jane Gruffydd had thought of the matter from that point of view; she had been thinking of the shame, people talking about them and some even rejoicing in their misfortune. But this was another worry. As soon as a new piece of gossip came along to take its place, the talk about them would die down, but the knotty problem of Sioned and her child would remain with the

Ffridd Felen family. Once she'd started looking ahead, the mother couldn't stop herself anticipating further problems.

'Well, now,' she said, 'we'll have to make sure that Twm hears nothing of this until his exams are over.'

'Yes,' said Elin, 'though it'll be hard to keep it from him because there are so many lads from the town in College. But I can go to Arthur and get him to swear not to say a word.'

'Yes, that's a good idea.'

'Because Twm is already so set against her,' said Elin.

And now at last she had the chance to tell her mother the story of why Twm left Sioned's house.

'Dear me,' said Jane Gruffydd. 'Who knows how often she's gone hungry because of that little scoundrel.'

'That wouldn't do her any harm,' said Elin, 'she stuffed herself with good food when she was at home. It's the little boy who's worst off; he'll be brought up in total chaos, I expect.'

'Well,' said Jane Gruffydd, 'there's no use talking; I'll just have to go down and see her.'

'Wait until tomorrow, so that you can get transport to take you there. I'll go there today, and you stay home to talk over with Dad what's the best thing to do.'

'No,' said Jane Gruffydd, 'I'll come down with you. I can't wait here all afternoon, and there's no use sending to the quarry for your father, and we can't keep on taking advantage of your mistress's kindness either.'

She went off to get ready.

'Look,' she said, 'since Twnt i'r Mynydd is too far, I'll just pop over and tell Jane Williams what's happened, and she can tell Ifan if he arrives home before I do. Everyone is bound to find out, so I might as well go and tell her myself. There'll be fewer lies mixed up with the news that way.'

Watching her mother come out through Jane Williams's gate Elin could not help but notice that she was shattered, and as she turned away from the gate there was a look of shock on her face.

Jane Gruffydd went to see Sioned by herself. Her legs were shaking by the time she reached her daughter's house, after having walked down all the way through the intense heat. She thought about her journeys into town; not one of them was ever without some trouble or other. This was a different kind of trouble, and a lot worse than the worries about the price of pigs and things like that.

Sioned and Eric were having tea with some unknown woman. Sioned's face changed for a minute on seeing her mother.

'Oh, you've got company,' she said.

'This is Bert's mother,' said Sioned.

Jane Gruffydd didn't really know what to make of Bert's mother. She was wearing earrings and several rings on her fingers – fingers which were quite dirty, whatever the state of her ears might have been. She didn't look as if she was particularly worried about her son. She carried on eating normally, making a clicking noise with her false teeth from time to time. She was wearing slippers with holes in them on her feet, which she tapped on the floor as she ate. Then she sat back in the armchair, and Jane Gruffydd noted that there wasn't much of a distance between her armpits and her waist, if she could be said to have a waist.

Sioned reached for a cup and poured some tea for her mother.

'This is a right pickle,' said Jane Gruffydd to herself, 'I'd better not say a word.'

'Did you walk down, Mrs Gruffydd?' said Mrs Ellis,

Bertie's mother.

'Yes, indeed, in this heat, and I left my washing half-done too.'

'Really, there was no need for you to come in such a hurry.'

'No, as you can see, I'm here to look after her.'

'Well, I thought she'd like to see her mother.'

'Oh, Janet* will get fair play,' said Bertie's mother.

'From who?' said Jane Gruffydd suddenly. 'It's clear that she won't be getting fair play from her husband.'

'Oh, yes she will; you'll see – Bertie will come back,' said his mother.

'If he's coming back, why did he go off in the first place?' asked Jane Gruffydd.

'You see, Mrs Gruffydd,' said Bert's mother, 'people tell lies – nobody tells the truth these days. I think Bert's gone away on business, as he said in his note.'*

'I hope so, indeed, but what about the money from Davies and Johnson?'

'Oh, don't talk to me about Davies and Johnson,' said Bert's mother, 'they're a suspicious* lot. (Jane Gruffydd didn't know what the English word 'suspicious' meant.) Perhaps it's just that a little mistake has been made.'

'I hope so, indeed,' said Jane Gruffydd.

'Oh, I'm sure of it, Mrs Gruffydd,' said Bert's mother, rubbing her soft, ringed fingers on the arms of the chair, and crossing her legs. 'Nobody knows Bert better than his own mother.' And she gave an emphatic click of her false teeth.

As if by instinct Jane Gruffydd stared at her own left hand, her wedding ring shining after being through the soap suds, and the skin of her hand shiny for the same reason, though blue, swollen veins stood out on the back.

She turned the ring around her finger with her thumb, as she always did when she was in a quandary. She hadn't yet decided whether she would ask Sioned to come home with her or not. She would like to have talked to Ifan about it first. But seeing Bert's mother there, swaggering about and lording it in the armchair, she didn't want her to assume that she thought more of her son than Jane did of her daughter, and she wanted to show her that Sioned had just as good a home and parents as Bertie did.

'Would you like to come home for a bit, you and Eric?' asked Jane Gruffydd.

'Oh, there's no need for you to bother, Mrs Gruffydd. I'll do my best for Janet,' said Mrs Ellis, butting in before Sioned could say anything.

But Sioned took no notice of her mother-in-law; she turned to her mother and said:

'No, I won't come up now for a little while, at least. I have to be here when Bertie comes back.'

Well, there's a lot of sense in that,' said her mother, 'but we'll see. But since Mrs Ellis is here with you, I'll try to get home before your father gets back from the quarry.'

'Will you be able to get a lift?' said Mrs Ellis.

'Not on a Monday like this.'

'Look, Grandma,' said Eric, who was standing beside the sewing machine by this time, 'Look what I've got.'

'Bring it here for your grandma to see,' said Jane Gruffydd.

And he ran over to show her his little train. 'Daddy's going to bring me back a tricycle.'

'Is he indeed? Well, here you are,' said his country grandma, and thrust sixpence into his hand.

'Tankyou,' said Eric, without biting the coin this time.

Jane Gruffydd was luckier than usual on her way back. She got a lift for most of the way with the vet, who was going in that direction.

She lit a fire and fried up some bacon and eggs before Ifan arrived home, and she let her husband eat his meal before telling him the news. As usual, Ifan Gruffydd was crestfallen. He was too stunned to be able to say much. He didn't move from the house for the rest of the evening. He was supposed to have gone to harvest the first growth of grass* for the cattle, but he let them do what they could with the remains of the poor grass until the following day. He was thinking about what the people in the quarry would say, and was worrying that the money he had earned had gone to the dogs, and to foreign dogs at that.* Seeing her husband so quiet, Jane thought that there was no point in them both worrying so much.

'Look,' she said, 'I've decided that I'm not going to fret about this any more.'

'But how is it possible not to?' he said.

'By remembering that something worse could have happened,' she said. 'Sioned could have died.'

'Perhaps that would have been less painful.'

'No indeed; we would have been worrying about a hundred and one things then – that we hadn't tried to help her sooner, and things like that.'

'Sioned has only ever brought us pain.'

'True enough, but this isn't her fault.'

'It was her fault that she married that little worm.'

'Perhaps, but very few people really know each other before they get married. A lot of men would like to escape from their wives if they were able to.'

'But Bertie didn't just run away from Sioned.'

'Well, whatever he was running away from, he's gone now.'

They sat together by the fire for a long time, without lighting the lamp. After a sultry, overcast day, the sun put in an appearance in the late afternoon, and went down over the Atlantic like a ball of fire, which just peeped its head up over the horizon before sinking at last into the water.

'We'd better go to bed, and we'll see what tomorrow brings,' said Jane.

At that, a low knock came at the door and Geini came in, peering to try to make them out in the darkness, where they sat like shadows under the great chimney.

'More suffering, Geini,' said Jane.

'Well, yes,' said she.

'Is it true that he's run off with some girl?'

'Is that what people are saying?'

'That's what I heard on the way here.'

'No, he hasn't,' said Ifan with some authority. 'All we know is that he's run off and that there's some mistake in the accounts.'

'Have you been into town, then?' his sister asked him.

'No, it was me who went,' Jane said, and she started to tell her story, including a description of Bertie's mother.

'They're some sort of riff-raff, then, bound to be,' said Geini.

'Yes. I certainly felt that I could look down my nose at her!'

Geini and Ifan laughed.

The two of them felt better after Geini's visit.

Bertie never did come back. Everyone assumed that he'd gone to America.

What would become of Sioned and Eric was the

161

problem that worried everyone most. It was the only thing that vexed Twm and Owen. William lived too far away and his visits home were too brief for the thing to affect him much. The two other boys dreaded that their holidays in Ffridd Felen would be spoilt if Sioned and her child came to live there. And who would keep her? But neither of the two dared to say anything about it in a letter beforehand. They knew too well of their mother's soft heart and practical kindness and they also knew how much she hated others interfering in anything which had to do with her personally.

It was Elin who settled the problem in the end. Whenever she had a night off, she would go and see Sioned and she watched her getting poorer and poorer. Sioned seemed utterly passive and without any vision of the future, except that she talked pathetically all the time about waiting for Bert to come back.

'Well, you could be waiting for him for years,' Elin said, 'It's obvious that his family aren't going to do anything for you, and it would be too much to ask Mam and Dad to do anything to help you.'

'I wouldn't go and live in the country again if you paid me to!'

'Well, since you think the town has been so good to you,' said Elin, 'you'd better ask it to help.'

'How do you mean?'

'Well, I'd sell this furniture, and I'd rent a little room somewhere to set myself up as a seamstress. I'll talk to my mistress, and ask her to have a word with her friends so that they'll bring you work to do.'

'What will I do with Eric?'

'Perhaps he'll be able to go home for a bit, until you earn enough to be able to keep your own house again.'

162

And that's what was agreed in the end.

By the time William and Owen came home in the holidays Eric was already there, looking a lot healthier and better turned out, and enjoying life with the other children in the district. Twm was at home a month earlier than the other two, and he had pretty much got used to his nephew. But, at first, he was very annoyed with his mother for taking Eric in, and he showed his disapproval by being touchy with his nephew. He couldn't stand the noise he made running around with his toys along the slate paving.

'Go and play somewhere else,' he would tell the boy, tetchily. This was about the sixth time his mother had heard him snap at the boy.

'Now then,' she said, 'nobody's going to be nasty to this little boy while he's here with us. If he's going to be living here, he's to be left alone, without anybody resenting him being here or taking it out on him.'

Twm was cut to the quick and went outside to cry. He had been working hard preparing for his exams after having neglected his work throughout the year, since he'd been reading all sorts of things which were nothing to do with the course.

21

When William came home in 1913, he brought his wife with him: it was the dark-eyed girl who had teased him when he was shy about taking his bath in a tub in front of the fire when he first went down South. In the same year, Twm gained a second class honours degree in Welsh. He failed to get a job in a County School and, rather than be out of work altogether, he took a post in a Primary School in Llan Ddôl,* which was quite close to home. He had to live for half a year on a salary less than that normally paid to a qualified teacher, since he hadn't gained teaching experience before going to College. He was fairly happy during the vacations. The fact that he had got a job at all was heartening. Owen thought he would be bound to get a post in a County School after gaining experience in a Primary School, as long as he didn't stay there too long.

These were the happiest holidays Jane and Ifan Gruffydd had enjoyed since Owen had first left to go to College. From now on, Jane wouldn't have to spend any money on any of the boys. She would have an opportunity to speed up the paying off of her bills in the shops.

Nobody in Ffridd Felen knew anything of William's marriage until a fortnight before he came home. And that was a good thing, because it gave Jane Gruffydd less time to ponder what kind of person her daughter-in-law would be. And, as it turned out, from the moment they clapped eyes on her, everyone loved Polly. Her eyes were blacker than bilberries but with a hint of blue in the whites, and her hair was as black and sleek as a crow's feathers. Ffridd Felen and Moel Arian were to her like a new toy to a child, with some new revelation lurking in every corner. It was all unfamiliar to someone who had been born and raised in the midst of terraced houses and the din of the coal mines. She talked incessantly, whether anyone understood her dialect or not, and she laughed openly, showing her little tongue, at anything in the dialect of her husband's family that she failed to understand. She got up early, helped her mother-in-law, and showed clearly that she didn't want her own and William's presence there on their holiday to mean more work for anyone. Indeed, there was less work for everyone because of Polly; when she saw work to be done, she did it without having to be asked.

Sioned came up over the Bank Holiday, and Polly worked more but talked less, since Sioned amazed her. Sioned had made a good start on her sewing business by this time, and this showed in her own clothes rather than in any offers of help towards Eric's keep. Tight skirts had begun to be fashionable, and Sioned's was so tight that she could barely walk. Between the high white collar of her blouse, and the little hat which tipped forward over her face like a toadstool, she looked very grand. She was like a queen to Polly, but the latter breathed more easily once she'd left.

One Saturday, Ifan and Jane Gruffydd, William, Polly,

and Eric went to Lleyn to visit the older generation in Sarn Goch. Polly was the one who came up with the idea for the jaunt. That was one thing she couldn't understand about her mother-in-law and the people of Moel Arian generally – they were so lacking in initiative. She was always telling her mother-in-law that she was stuck in the house far too much.

'But where shall I go?' said Jane Gruffydd.

'Anywhere, it doesn't matter where.'

So she and William planned the trip to Sarn Goch one Saturday, and they paid for everyone to go with them.

Jane Gruffydd would often look back on that Saturday. It was the last time that she saw her parents alive. Her father and mother would both be dead and buried within the year. But Jane had the chance to tell her mother that she was beginning to turn the corner now, and she was able to pay back the money that she had borrowed from her from time to time.

'There's no need for you to do that,' her mother had said. 'I'm not long for this world, and you might as well keep that money as have us leave it to you again after we've gone.'

And that's exactly how it was in the will.

When the summer holidays of 1914 came around, Polly wasn't able to suggest a trip to Lleyn, and the War prevented them taking any trips anywhere else.

When the War broke out, nobody in Moel Arian knew what to make of it really. They didn't understand its causes, but believed what the papers said, that Great Britain was going to the aid of small countries that were being trampled upon. But they felt the effects of the war from the very first day, since all the small quarries in the neighbourhood closed down; indeed, one of them closed down even before the War was announced. But War was something for soldiers and politicians; all they knew was that the price of everything would go up, and they told the story of the old lady who put up the price of mints during the Franco-Prussian War. The Ffridd Felen children could remember the Boer War. They remembered how the Primary School headmaster had made them march through the village waving banners when Mafeking was relieved, but that meant absolutely nothing to them. One or two people belonged to the volunteer militia, but that was hardly something to be proud of. On the contrary, people tended to pour scorn on members of the militia, and they did the same when the first military uniform was seen in Moel Arian in 1914, although its colour was different from that of the militia soldier's.

Neither Owen nor Twm felt that there was any danger that the War would affect them in any way. William and Polly went back without having travelled around the district much. There was nothing to put your finger on to account for this, except for a general feeling of unease.

Twm was still teaching in the Primary School at Llan Ddôl. He had failed time and time again to get a post in a County School. He got as far as the shortlist in one place, and the headmaster there had told him, as he explained that he wasn't offering him the job, that he would be better off giving up his current post, since teaching for a long time in a Primary School was more of a hindrance than a help in getting a post in a County School. But that was impossible now, with his father out of work once more.

So back he went again, with a slight incentive of a pound a month extra in his pay packet this time. That was little enough of a consolation, considering how much he hated his work. He didn't like teaching children at the best of times. But teaching them in the circumstances of Llan

Ddôl was hell for him. He taught a class of sixty children in the same room as another class of sixty, taught by another two teachers. The entrance to the infants' class was under the window of his room, and four times a day the infants went out during the end of his lessons. The worst thing of all was that the headmaster's desk was in the same room, and so he was under the hawk's eye all the time. The headmaster beat the children mercilessly. They were sent there from other classes, and the children in Twm's class had to watch others being punished continually. Every morning, soon after he led the prayers in assembly, the headmaster would beat the latecomers with a long cane. Twm boiled inside at the injustice of the thing. The hawk would descend suddenly on his own class all the time, just because he was in a bad mood, not with the children, but about something else. And to top everything, Twm wasn't able to make use of his knowledge of Welsh, but was forced to teach subjects which he knew nothing about.

As 1914 wore on, more of the grey uniforms were seen about the place. There was a busyness all through the land, and changes happening from one day to the next. And there was a stirring in Twm's blood. He wanted to be able to come and go, and he didn't have enough money to do that after sending some of it home. There was nothing to do in Llan Ddôl. Sometimes he went to Bangor at the weekend to see Ceinwen, who was in her third year at College, and he also saw some of his peers among the College lads. Every time he went there he heard about boys from his year who had joined the army, and those who were still students were joining up in droves.

On a Friday in January 1915, the School was more hateful than ever. It had been pouring with rain all day, and

Twm's classroom was full of damp smells of clothes drying. The children weren't allowed out to play at three o'clock, but they weren't allowed to go home any earlier either. Twm decided to go to Bangor, though he had been there the previous weekend. The lure of joining up was getting stronger all the time. By the time he reached Bangor that night, he found that Arthur, his old Schoolfriend, had abandoned his research and had joined up. On Saturday morning the entrance hall of the College was half-empty, and there was no conversation to be had with anyone except the girls, who were themselves full of fuss and enthusiasm about somebody or other having joined up, though a few of them were sad. That night Twm and two of his friends who were still at College, Bob Huws and Dai Morgan, went to the Black Lion and there, over their pints, the three of them decided that they would join the army, and to seal their bargain they drank more beer, and Twm composed an *englyn* to his headmaster. They went back to their lodgings blind drunk, and Twm slept on the sofa in the parlour. By the following day they were repentant, but Twm felt the attraction returning as Monday morning came closer.

On Monday morning, the headmaster came to him and showed him a mistake that he had made in the attendance register the previous Friday afternoon. The smells of that afternoon came back to Twm, and he remembered the circumstances in which he had added those figures together. The blood rose to his head. He threw his chalk on the desk, put on his coat and walked out of the School without giving a single lesson that morning. He didn't look back; otherwise, if he had caught sight of the disappointed look on the faces of some of the girls in the front row he might have changed his mind.

There was adventure in the air, and the world was too small for him. He kept bumping his elbows against its walls. But those walls were coming down this morning. He would get to see the world, and to see something apart from these eternal mountains and the sour face of the headmaster.

22

On Thursday morning, as Eric was putting on his cap ready to go to School, he heard the postman at the gate and he ran to meet him.

'A letter, Grandma. Ta-ta, I'm off now.'

'Ta-ta. I wonder who the letter can be from today. It's Twm's writing but the postmark.... Have you seen my glasses anywhere, Ifan?'

'Here they are.'

Jane sat down on a chair, her face white.

'What's the matter?' said Ifan.

'Read that.' And his lips began to tremble. He walked to the door, leant on the doorpost and looked out towards Anglesey.

When he came back, his wife was crying.

'Oh,' she said, 'children can be cruel.'

'Yes, they can,' he said, looking thoughtfully into the fire. 'I think it'll be best for me to go and look for work somewhere.'

'No,' she said, 'you'd better not – not for a while, anyway.'

'I don't see how we can go on like this.'

'It's been worse for us before.'

'I don't know – prices are still going up and up.'

'But the prices of other things will follow,' she said, 'pigs and so on, and we don't have anyone to keep now except Eric.'

'And Sioned should be giving us something for his keep now.'

'Yes she should, but we ought to know Sioned by now.'

The following week, Twm's clothes and books were delivered from Llan Ddôl. His mother folded his clothes and put them in a drawer in his bedroom. She took some of the dishes off the lowest shelf of the dresser in the parlour, and put his books there instead. She leafed through them but didn't understand them. At the end of the month they received five pounds from Twm, which was his final salary for the work he'd done. She put the money in a box to keep until he came home.

When Owen heard about Twm's decision, he was beside himself with anger, but he didn't write to him while he was in that frame of mind. His own salary had stayed the same even though prices were going up and up. His landlady had already said that she would be asking for eleven shillings a week for his two rooms. And here was Twm playing such a dirty trick! When he could have been sending money home, he'd gone and joined the soldiers, where he wouldn't be getting enough for the luxuries that he wanted. It was true that his headmaster was nasty, and that he deserved a much better post, and yet ... he should have thought about his father and mother. Then he recalled the conversation they had had the first Christmas after he had got the job in Tre Ffrwd, and how Twm had said that it was possible to worry too much about family. Twm hadn't showed that he worried much at all. But it wasn't just that he'd got fed up with helping his family, all the same. No; Owen remembered his restlessness in the town, and his longing to see and find out and know about things for himself, not just learning about them in books. The world was too narrow for him. He could never sit down quietly in the house after composing a *cywydd*.*

'Come for a walk to the top of the mountain,' he had said once in Ffridd Felen, after writing a poem, 'so that we can get some room to move our feet about.' He remembered that walk now. The lapwing calling. Moonlight reflected in the peaty water. The lamps of the town like a cluster of jewels by the riverside. The lights of Holyhead coming and going on the horizon, and the summit of Snowdon a clear sprig jutting up into the moonlight.

Before Owen could write, he received a letter from Twm written from somewhere in the English border counties. He didn't sound entirely happy, and the main reason for that was, as far as Owen could make out, that Bob Huws and Dai Morgan had not kept to their word, and had refused to go with Twm to join up. He had almost gone back to the School, but he knew that the door would be locked against him there. He was surrounded by strangers. Owen didn't have the heart to tell him off in his letter. Nobody believed that the War would last very long, and no one had an inkling that those who joined up now would be sent abroad.

The summer holiday of 1915 was a troubled one for Jane Gruffydd. William and Polly were in Ffridd Felen, and they had a six-month-old baby girl with them this time. Owen was at home, and Bet visited for a while. Owen was utterly at a loss without Twm, and he had no money to go travelling anywhere. Bet talked of going away to work in a munitions factory. Twm had been mentioning for a while in his letters that he was expecting to be allowed a visit home, and that it could happen any day, or it could be postponed until September. His mother didn't really know which she would prefer. She longed to see him, and yet she would like to have him with her when there was less bustle and commotion.

She and Eric, Ifan, William, Polly and the baby went over to Anglesey one Saturday. For the life of her Jane Gruffydd couldn't stop herself comparing the day with their previous visit to Lleyn two years before. They could see Moel Arian and the quarries across the water. She longed to be back there, and to have a cup of hot, fresh tea in her own house. But she dared not suggest going back. Ifan looked completely out of place, somehow. She had had enough of the entirely natural racket made by William and Polly while playing with the baby, and of watching Eric hurling stones into the water. But they could go home no sooner, since the steamer and these newfangled motors which had started to travel back and forth to Moel Arian were infrequent. By the time they reached the town and went to the Square, there was a large crowd of people there waiting to be ferried in every direction, and swarming amongst them everywhere were soldiers in their grey uniforms, some by themselves, some talking and flirting with young girls. They stood and waited for the motor bus to arrive.

In front of them was a tall soldier with his back to them, and Polly said 'Look, there's a fine-looking soldier.'

The soldier turned his head and grinned at them.

'Twm!' exclaimed everyone all together.

As they walked the last mile home after the trip in the

bus, Jane Gruffydd took note of the big difference between Twm's gait and that of his father.

Those days flew by like the wind, and Twm slipped from his mother's grip in the same way. She couldn't get used to seeing him in that old uniform. He couldn't be persuaded that he could get away with wearing normal clothes. To her, he wasn't Twm in that uniform. And yet it was Twm who talked and laughed and ate. She couldn't manage to get him on his own as she used to when he came home for weekends from Llan Ddôl. There were lots of people around the table at every mealtime, and so she couldn't urge him to eat as much as he could.

She made some pickled herring from the little fishes that you get in August. They ate them with new potatoes and oaten bread and buttermilk.

'Oh,' said Twm, groaning after he had finished eating, 'that food was so good.'

'Do you get decent food in the army?' asked his mother.

'That would be a real feast there,' he said.

And so the days went by.

Twm said as he prepared to leave, 'If you get ten minutes to mix up a cake, remember me.'

It was then that it dawned on his mother that she could express her feelings by sending food to her son.

He came home again at Christmas, and he and Owen had countless conversations together. More people in the district had joined up by this time, and in the Literary Festival there were lots of soldiers, children from the area who were at home for a visit. And yet, nobody there thought for a minute that any of them would see any actual fighting. It was while he was talking to Twm that the first inkling of danger came over Owen. Yes, Twm was almost certain that he was going to be sent abroad. He was fed up with being in this country by now, he said, and he hoped to be sent to Egypt or somewhere in the Far East. Since his father and mother didn't seem to be aware of this possibility, Owen thought it wiser not to enlighten them. Indeed, Twm's training had gone on so long by now that his parents thought he would carry on training until the end of the War.

In May, Twm came home without a word of warning, and he explained that he had swapped his leave with someone else and so had arrived unexpectedly. Twm was as cheerful as he usually was but he seemed to have no inclination to go and visit anybody. He mooched about the house, and helped his father in the fields, and since nobody was at home except him, his mother was able to stroll about the fields at his side. New, dark green potato shoots were poking out of the soil, the new hay was beginning to ripen, and the first growth of grass was already green and thick.* His father and mother had plenty of time to spend with him, watching the hen and her newly-hatched chicks. They were so sweet running after their mother through the grass, like little lumps of yellow, and the three of them laughed heartily at them. Twm felt that he would like to take each of them up in both hands. Occasionally one of them would try to spread its pathetic little wings so comically.

But in the chapel on Sunday evening Twm felt quite downhearted. His mother was there (she seldom went to church now), along with his father, Eric, and himself. The chapel doors stood open, and there filtered inside the sad bleating of lambs and the crowing of a cockerel somewhere far in the distance. It was a prayer meeting, and Twm always knew what to expect next from some of the prayer leaders. But he felt a shiver of fear when he heard some of the old ones adding: 'And remember the boys who are away fighting on land and sea.' The singing was poor, since so many of the men were away. One of the deacons referred at the end of the service to 'Thomas Gruffydd', saying that they were glad to see him home and looking so well, and wherever he should be sent in future, they hoped to see him again, and may God protect him in the meantime. As he went out, Twm noticed that there wasn't the usual knot of people in the chapel porch, nor was there a rush for the door as there used to be.

'And how are you keeping now?'

'You're looking well.'

'I hope you don't get sent abroad.'

It was late by the time Twm was able to escape, and he hurried home, having a race with Eric. He looked forward to his supper. He knew that they would be having cold meat and fried potatoes. And one thing he liked about Sunday nights was, even if they arrived home at seven, they would get their supper as soon as they got there. Eric thought the world of his uncle Twm and was proud to walk beside him. He loved to watch him polish his buttons and put his cap on just so.

'Pity old Now* isn't here with us too,' thought Twm as he ate his supper. It would be impossible to see him this time but – so what! – he'd be sure to see him again before long.

On the fourth day he had to go back. He had one more day off but he wanted to go and see Ceinwen on his way back. He thought sometimes about telling his mother about Ceinwen, but he didn't know how she would react, and there would be plenty of time to tell her some other time; and perhaps some other Ceinwen would end up being his wife. If he told his mother that he had five days' leave, he was sure she'd be hurt if he didn't spend it all at home.

He seemed quite unconcerned to be going back. He sang some of the songs that he'd learned at the camp, much to Eric's delight.

'When are you coming back again, Uncle Twm?'

'Haymaking time.'

'Is that a long time?'

'No, no time at all. Ta-ta, Eric.'

'Ta-ta.'

'I wouldn't mind coming to the station with you to send you on your way,' said his mother. 'These motor buses are so handy.'

'Yes, why don't you come, then?' he said.

'And look,' she said, 'I kept your last pay packet. It's there for you. Take some of it with you now.'

That was when he came closest to breaking down.

'Well, alright, I'll take a pound,' he said, 'you spend more money in the summer – but you have the rest.'

'No; it'll still be there for you when you come back again.'

'Well, goodbye now then, Father.'

'And you, Twm, and good luck.'

'I'll see you again at haymaking time, for sure.'

'Very good, and let's hope this old War will be over by then.'

Twm regretted in a way letting his mother come to see him off in town. Saying goodbye became a long-drawn-out affair, and he would have preferred to say goodbye to her while she was in her apron at home than to see her there in the town station and to think about her long, lonely journey back to Moel Arian. But, as she had said, the motor buses were handy by this time.

At the station he wanted to hold her hand, but he didn't. He put his head out of the window, and went on looking at her walking up the platform. When she reached the far end, she turned around and looked at him, and waved; he raised his hand too, and went on watching her until the bridge hid her from view. He noticed how old-fashioned her skirt and coat were as she stood there at the far end of the platform.

In a few days Owen received a letter from Twm confirming his fears that he was going to be posted overseas:

'...I had hoped to get to see you, but it wasn't possible. I had only five days, and I spent four of them at home and one with Ceinwen; I didn't tell them at home that I had five, so as not to hurt their feelings. I thought once that I should send for you, but Dad and Mam would have twigged then that I was on my last leave. They looked fairly contented; I don't think they suspected at all that I was going to be sent away, and Eric is a great solace to them now. We went to visit Elin, and Bet, *and Sioned*. I was feeling soft and forgiving at the time, and the pieces of my old life don't seem to fit into this new life of mine, somehow. Sioned seems to be flourishing. She has plenty of work, remodelling shop-bought clothes for people, and she's as pretty as ever. She was glad to see us.

'This camp is pandemonium at the moment; everyone packing madly and cursing loudly. I can hardly credit that I was in the peace and quiet of Moel Arian only three days ago. Everywhere was incredibly beautiful. I hadn't realized till now that it's years since I'd been at home in May. I hated having to leave, but I expect if it had been peacetime and I actually had to live there, I wouldn't see anything in it. It was lovely to have plenty of time to watch a hen and her chicks and to feel the heat starting to rise up from the earth. There was peace and quiet to do anything you liked, and very few people around. Isn't it a shame that we don't always have plenty of time like that to stand and stare at things like chickens and sheep and dogs, and not to have to worry about anything at all?

'I went up to the top of the mountain one night, but it wasn't quite the same as when we two went up after I'd written that *cywydd*. I remembered lots of things that Bet and I used to do when we were children – catching minnows, stringing bilberries on a blade of grass and eating them (I can feel the harsh texture of the grass between my teeth right now), and tugging marsh clubmoss* out of the ground, having a contest to see who could pick the longest strand of it, and then plaiting it around our heads.

'I'm looking at my bed in this cabin now; it's been my bed for months, and though it wasn't as comfortable as my bed at home, I liked it a lot, and it was heaven to turn into it when I was tired out. Have you ever thought how adorable a bed is? But someone else will be sleeping in this one tonight. I wonder who? Someone nice perhaps, or maybe a right scoundrel. It makes no odds. That person will have to leave it again one day, and someone else will take his place, but I'll be sorry to think of that tonight, wherever I shall be.

'John Twnt i'r Mynydd has joined up as well – he had had quite enough of his boss. The man was working him into the ground, and resurrecting stuff that had been in the shop since before the flood to sell for exorbitant prices. Well, let the shopkeepers rake in the money!

'I don't know where I'm going. I had hoped to go to the East, but now I'd be just as happy to go to France. If I'm wounded, I could come home. Whoa, there goes a boot sailing past my head! I hope to be able to see you before long.

"Farewell, now, until that lovely day
when we'll see each other, come what may".*

Yours as always, Twm.'

23

When Jane and Ifan Gruffydd heard that Twm was in France, it was a great blow to them. They had not imagined for one minute that he would have to go. They still believed that the War would be over before boys like Twm would have to go.

From then on, a cloud hung over their heads all the time, and they felt as if they were just waiting for it to burst. Somehow, they didn't believe it was possible for the sun to chase the cloud away. Their worst agony was waiting for the postman to bring a letter. After receiving one they would be happy for a few days; then they would start to worry once more.

The mother made cakes, and sent parcels to France twice a week. That was the only thing she did in the week that she put her whole soul into, and it was a depressing thing for her to see her husband bringing cigarettes to include in the parcel, since he himself was so set against them. The neighbours did the same.

'Since you're sending a parcel, put these cigarettes in for Twm,' they would say.

So they called by often, until their own children joined the army.

There was no work at all to be had in Moel Arian. The young and middle-aged men either joined the army or went to the munitions factories, or to work on the docks in Liverpool and other ports. Ifan Gruffydd would go and get work unloading cargoes from ships in Holyhead from time to time, and then he would return to do things on the farm. He was able to come home at weekends when he was working there. By now it was a blessing to have Eric with them. And the people who were left at home began to question themselves and each other about the meaning of it all. The world had often been harsh for them. They had suffered hardship and injustice in the quarries; oppression by masters and owners, the oppression of favouritism and corruption. They had seen their friends and children killed at work, but they had never had their children taken away from them to be killed in a war before. They tried to explain the thing in every way possible in the Sunday School now, since there was no quarry cabin to debate in any longer.

They did not believe at all by this time that the reason for the War was to right the wrong done to small countries, nor that this was the war to end all wars, nor that one country was to be blamed for it more than the others. But they did come to believe that there were people in every country who welcomed war, and that these people were using the sons of Moel Arian for their own advantage. These were 'the bigwigs', those same people who crushed them in the quarry, and who sucked their blood and turned it into gold for themselves. In the core of their being, they now believed that some were making money out of the War, as they made money out of their bodies in the quarries, and that these people sought to delay the end of the War. But they also knew, if their children refused to go, that they would be sure to come and fetch them and compel them to go.

The big problem for them in the Sunday School was why, if God existed, he did not intervene? Why did he allow the poor to suffer always? Just as there were shifts and changes in the wider world, so did their own opinions shift and change. Their faith in preachers and leaders was shaken. Preachers who had been like gods to them before now stood condemned by them because they were in favour of the War. Indeed, some stayed away from chapel for months because a preacher had talked of the righteousness of this War. In the same way, other preachers rose in their estimation for preaching its injustice. They were unanimous on one thing: the names of some famous political leaders began to stink to high heaven.

But the War went on. More and more boys came home in uniform, and news of deaths began to filter through.

In Tre Ffrwd, Owen was worrying as usual. The same things were going through his mind. He was thoroughly fed up with the daft, empty talk that he heard everywhere, even from people who were supposed to be clever. In that small, proud town he heard people talk about the glory of war and the boys' valour, and they believed every word they read in the newspapers. It was true that they worked hard to send comfort parcels to the soldiers and to welcome them when they came home and so on, but the soft, empty talk and the stereotypical ideas they expressed endlessly were enough to send anyone completely mad. Their children came home from the training camps, and if they were officers they would turn their noses up at a man like Owen who dared to walk the streets still wearing his own civilian clothes. Owen thought it was all very well for those boys, the boys from the grammar Schools, who had been pampered throughout their lives, and had never known want; if they suffered hardship now, it was for the very first time in their lives. As for his own people, they had experienced hardship throughout their lives and, as if they hadn't had enough, war came along like an unseen fist and crushed them into the ground. He had the urge to go up to the stiff, immaculate officers and tell them all this. But what would be the point? How could they, in the midst of their plenty, in the fertile valley of their lives, ever know or understand a little place like Moel Arian, with its thin crust of soil, which was too poor to keep cattle like theirs? What did they know of struggling to survive and snatching a living by force from a land of peat bog and clay? Though sometimes that land did produce a crop of brains.

Some of the female teachers in the School took to reproaching him for not joining up. He was too contemptuous of them to bother explaining that he had been excused for the present for reasons of ill health. The only thing that would make him join would be his feeling of solidarity with his friends and relatives who had already joined up. He felt that if they were suffering, he should be there suffering with them, not because of his sympathy with the War but because of his sympathy with the boys. This bothered him more and more as the letters came from Twm; not that his brother complained. The absence of complaint, when he knew that there was plenty of cause to complain, made him feel that he ought to go and share the suffering with Twm. And then he remembered about his parents at home. He knew very well how they were feeling there, and if he should join up, he knew how they

185

would feel then. But the next minute he would feel that his responsibility towards Twm was greater.

In the School there was a young teacher called Ann Ellis, a girl from Meirionethshire. Owen had never exchanged more than a 'Good Morning' with her. She was exceptionally quiet, and some days she looked unbearably sad. One day she received a telegram which told her that her sweetheart had been killed in the War. When she came back after a few days, she looked like someone who had been ill for months. Owen wanted to go to her and tell her how sorry he was, but she walked past him and everyone else without saying a word.

Within a month a telegram came summoning Owen home, and there was no need for anyone to tell him why.

That morning, at the start of July, 1916, Jane Gruffydd was expecting a letter from Twm. She hadn't received one for six days. She was very worried, but not overwhelmingly so, since his letters had been delayed like this before, and she had received two letters at once then. These days she couldn't do anything except milk the cow and get Eric ready for School before the postman came, though sometimes he would be late. On this day he was late, or perhaps he had already gone by. Yet she continued to sit and wait instead of getting up and making a start on her work. No; there was his whistle by the gate to the lane, and she ran towards him gladly. But it wasn't a letter from Twm, nor from any of her other children. It was a long letter with a government stamp on it.

'Drat it,' she said to herself, 'here's another old form to fill in with lots of questions. They must think we've got a thousand-acre farm.'

But when she opened it, she realized that it wasn't

that kind of document. These papers were in English. She saw Twm's name on them and his army number, and there was another thick sheet of white paper with just a small bit of English on it.

She ran to the shop with the letter.

'Richard Huws, here's an old letter in English come. Can you tell me what it is? It's something to do with Twm at any rate.'

The shopkeeper read it, and held it in his hand for a moment, saying nothing.

'Sit down, Jane Gruffydd,' he said, tenderly.

'What is it?' she said. 'Nothing's happened, has it?'

'Yes, I'm afraid it has,' he said.

'Is he still alive?'

'No he isn't, I'm afraid. Ann!' he called from the shop into the kitchen, 'bring a glass of water here now!'

'Come through into the kitchen, Jane Gruffydd,' said Ann, as she came and took her by the arm.

Later she went back with her to Ffridd Felen.

At that time Ifan was working for a few days on the haymaking at a farm not far away, where they started on the harvest earlier than in Moel Arian. When he saw a man crossing the field towards him, he knew instantly why he was being called home.

All the children arrived home before nightfall. The neighbours called and did the work that had to be done. Every kindness was shown. That night, after the door was closed on the last visitor, the children and their parents gathered together around the fire, feeling that was the way they should be on the night that the first gap had been made in the family.

As the mother put her head down on her pillow and

tried to close her eyes on the pain, dozens of sad thoughts came into her mind. But amidst them all there darted one other: that she would no longer have to fear the sound of the postman coming the next day.

24

Sudden, seismic shifts were going on in the world outside but in Ffridd Felen it was as if time stood still. It was like that for every family in the same circumstances, but nobody knew or cared about anyone else's sadness except their own. There was no tomorrow to look forward to. Only yesterday remained. The boys went on joining up, news came of their deaths, and a hymn was sung in their memory in chapel; and though they went from one family to the next to extend their sympathies, they all returned to the pain that awaited them on their own hearths.

The children got used to the airships that took off from the station on the mountain nearby.

The hay harvest came, normally a happy, joyful time, when the weather was good; a time for fun and laughter; and for children, a time of good food and having a whale of a time. But there was none of that in Ffridd Felen this year. It was mostly women in the hayfield; it was they who loaded and carried the hay. William didn't come this year, since he had only just been. Owen arrived home before they harvested the hay. He worked on the trailer or on top of the hayrick. He tried to behave as if nothing had happened. Everyone else did the same. Nobody talked about the reason for their grief. But it was the only thing at the back of everyone's mind.

Time dragged on in this way. The Christmas holidays came, and went. And oh, how everyone longed for them to be over.

Before Owen came home the following summer, John Twnt i'r Mynydd had been killed, and one of the hardest tasks Owen ever had to do was to visit his family. He remembered what a cheerful place Twnt i'r Mynydd had always been. It was the kind of house that was full of furniture and crockery and children and, as such, there was always room there for more children, someone else's children, and nobody ever felt that he would be in the way there. Ann Ifans had changed so completely that he felt for the first time ever that there was no welcome for him. But he tried to put himself in her place; a woman who had laughed her way through life, regardless of the cost of living or the price of animals, a woman who had never allowed such things to bother her at all; when the source of her joy was taken away from her – the boy who had in the past made her life a life of laughter – it was not surprising that she collapsed under the burden of it. Because Ann Ifans had lived a happy life so far; she was tidy, careful, and tried to pay her way, but none of it was ever a burden on her. She had enough common sense to see that there was no use being over-ambitious on behalf of her children, whatever other people's children did; but she enjoyed life with her husband and her children. They were allowed to play wherever they wanted to in the house and the sheds, they were allowed to borrow a rope to make a swing, they were allowed to climb trees, bring stuff into the house to build a kite; and not only that but their mother would sit down with them to help build the kite, and she would have the first go on the swing, and she joined them in concealing from their father the damage they had done to his ropes. It would have been hard for Ann Ifans ever to have punished her children but, somehow or other, there was never any call for her to do so.

As he was leaving, she said to Owen,

'You used to walk to town with John in days gone by, didn't you?'

'Yes,' he said, and he could think of nothing else to say.

'Come here again, Owen,' she said, 'come often; I will be pleased to see you.'

And when he did go back to visit, she talked about John all the time, and her theme every time was this,

'You see, Owen, he had a nasty, miserly master; he'd save up his own shit, if he could.'*

'The headmaster at Twm's School was a nasty old man too.'

'Goodness, I thought Twm was in a really nice place.'

'No; the Schoolmaster was very pernickety, and he half killed the children, and he'd kill the teachers too, if he could.'

'The poor boys,' she said.

Sometimes people would ask him to write letters for them to their children who were in the army. That wasn't difficult when he was familiar enough with the children, but if they were quite a bit younger than he was and he had lost track of them, it could be really difficult.

'What would you like to say to Huw, John Jones?'

'Oh, you say whatever you think is best.'

'Well, yes, I'll give him some of the local news but what do you want to say to him?'

'Say that his mother and I are thinking of him with all our hearts, and hoping that he's safe and that he'll come home soon.'

And that was all. They couldn't express their innermost thoughts.

The holidays went by slowly. There was nothing much to do. The weather was wet. Dark clouds hung above Anglesey every day. The fields were greeny-blue and the second growth of grass was thick. The purple of the heather and the yellow of the gorse were fresh and bright against the blackness of the mountains all around. There was no sign of the sun to brighten the rocks nor wilt the heather. Yet it was close and sultry for churning the butter, which stayed soft. His mother went on with her work the same as ever. She didn't mention Twm much, hardly showing her feelings, but Owen knew just from the way she held herself as she went about her work that the only thing on her mind was Twm. Sometimes she asked out of the blue,

'Do you think it would have been better for Twm to have gone back to College instead of taking that job in Llan Ddôl?'

'No, I don't; he would have joined the army even sooner then.'

'But perhaps he wouldn't have got killed.'

He knew too that she dusted his books in the parlour often, though he didn't catch her doing it.

He knew one other thing, too, namely that the fact that he was at home was a consolation to her. She showed no sign of this. But when the time came for him to go back, she started to show how she felt. She prepared food as always. She made lamb's head stew with the meat minced finely along with the liver. She made pickled herring in August, and they all had to admit that they enjoyed their food.

Eric was ten years old by this time, and a sensible lad for his age. He had cried along with his family when the news came about Uncle Twm, and he had realized later that talking about him was painful to his grandmother – that is, talking about him in the careless way of children.

Owen was sorry for Eric. It wasn't much fun for him to be all on his own in Ffridd Felen, though he did bring other children to play there often. In the summer holidays, though, he had nowhere to go, and he just trotted about the place in his heavy, dusty boots all day long. And yet, he supposed they themselves had done the same when they were children. No; it had been different for them – there had been a lot of them, there had been no war out there in the world, and Jane and Ifan Gruffydd had been younger.

'I'm going to take Eric for a trip somewhere,' he said to his mother one fine day, which put in an appearance during a gap in the eternal wet weather. 'You come too, and then perhaps Father will come.'

'No, I won't come,' said his mother, as if shocked that anyone should expect her to go anywhere, 'but Eric will be delighted. The poor little creature doesn't get to go anywhere.'

In Llandudno, the two of them sat on the beach all afternoon; Eric paddled in the sea, and had a generally perfect time.

'We'd better go and have some tea now, old man,' said Owen. 'What do you fancy?'

'Ice cream* and cake.'

'Alright, then – come on.'

As they walked up the street, Owen saw a motor car stopping opposite the cafe that he was aiming for, and a military officer getting out of it, and after him emerged his sister, Sioned.

Owen grabbed Eric's hand and turned him around to look in the opposite direction.

'What's up, Uncle Owen?'

'I've suddenly remembered that there's an excellent place for ice cream in this street here.'

'Better than that other place?'

'Oh yes, much better.'

Later on, while they were at the tea table:

'What's the matter, Uncle Owen? Don't you like the cake?'

'Yes, except that it's giving me toothache.'

'Try this one – it hasn't got any sugar on top.'

Owen was musing on what he had seen. He had seen his sister walking with a soldier before while wandering about the town. She had looked very handsome this afternoon. She was wearing a black and white suit and a black hat. She didn't look much older than when she had got married.

'Lucky the child didn't see her,' he said to himself, 'and I'll have to bite my tongue to stop myself mentioning it at home.'

'Right, Eric, what else do you want?'

'Nothing, thanks; I've eaten so much I'm nearly bursting.'

'Well, we'll go and look at the shops now, and we'll have a look at the little birds.'

'We've got to buy something for Grandpa and Grandma, haven't we, Uncle Owen?'

'Yes, you're right – lucky you remembered.'

'I remembered all the time since this morning, and I want to buy something for Llew too.'

'Who's Llew?'

'You know, that little boy in Jane Williams's house. She's his grandma.'

'Right – let's go.'

When they were sitting by the seaside once more, a pipe for Granddad, a little jug for Grandma, and a fishing net for Llew in their pockets, Owen asked,

'What would you like to do when you grow up, Eric?'

'I want to be a printer like Wmffra, Bryn Arian.'

'Would you like to go to School?'

'No, I'd rather play with my engine and stuff like that.'

'How do you know you'd like to be a printer?'

'Well, one day I went with Auntie Bet to see where Wmffra works, and Wmffra says I can go and be his apprentice. Mind you, I'll be coming home to sleep at Granddad and Grandma's house, and not at Mam's.'

'Oh, it's too soon to be deciding things like that.'

In September the weather turned fine, just when it was time for Owen to go back, which made it all the harder for him to come to terms with leaving. He went out some mornings to gather blackberries for his mother to make jam.

On the last Monday of his holiday he got up at about six and went out blackberry picking in Coed y Ceunant. In the silence and loneliness of the wood he had one of those terrible bouts of longing* that came upon him often since his brother's death. Everywhere was so still that the smooth rush of the stream seemed loud. If something scuffled among the trees, he jumped in alarm. As the heat of the sun increased, a haze began to rise off the sea. The late growth of grass was thick and dripping with dew. The outlines of the cattle that had been lying in the field before going off to be milked could be seen in light patches in the grass. He could almost feel the heat of the cow as he sat on a rock beside where she had been lying. He remembered all the times he had been blackberrying with his brother, after School usually. He could smell the scent of the trees as it had been in the clear air of a September evening, and he could see their pockets bulging with the nuts they had picked. The night would close about them suddenly, and they would run home with the sweat pouring from their brows, to be welcomed by their mother who was glad of the blackberries. He remembered how Twm could hardly wait for his mother to make the pudding that night. But he fell asleep before he could even get undressed. He remembered how they had enjoyed the pudding next day, and they had sat on the wall outside cracking nuts, exactly as Eric did nowadays. He remembered how warm and dark the kitchen was, and how good it was to be sitting on the wide stile on the wall outside.

But what was the point of dreaming? Those things belonged to some other life; yes, he would almost say that they were about some other people too. He began to feel hungry and he started for home, feeling as he always did when he had one of these bouts of longing for the past that he would like to wake up one day and find that it had all been a dream. And yet, he knew that it was his parents who had suffered the sharpest blow when Twm died.

But recently, after a bout like this, he had seen a chink of light. His life in the School wasn't as entirely monotonous as it had been. So far, Ann Ellis and he had been the only two among the teachers to have lost someone in the War. That fact grew to be a tie between them, and a friendship began; they could talk to each other now about things that they could never discuss with anyone else. They talked incessantly about the injustice of everything in those days and, more than anything else, how blind people were. They always felt better after having talked to each other. Thinking of this now was what brought a chink of light to Owen's black mood and he was able to lift himself out of the huge depression which threatened to overwhelm him.

When he reached the house there was a stranger there, and he discovered that he was a military pensions officer. A while ago he had made an application on his mother's behalf for her to get a small pension on account of Twm, on the same principle as the mothers of apprentices got a pension. The officer had called there with endlessly long forms which asked all sorts of questions: What was Twm's salary in the year that he had been a teacher? What was his father's salary and that of all the other children? How much money did they get out of farming Ffridd Felen?

The man shook his head doubtfully, as if to say that there was too much money coming in.

Jane Gruffydd said,

'There's no need for you to assume that I get money from any of the children except this one,' nodding at Owen, 'and to be honest, he shouldn't be sending us anything because his pay hasn't gone up at all as prices have risen. And if the price of butter and pigs has gone up, the animal feed has gone up in price too, and the interest rates have gone up too.'

'Well, the other children can help you.'

'No indeed they can't; the pay packets of two of the girls have hardly got any bigger at all, and my other son has got a family to keep.'

'Well, I'll see what I can do,' he said, putting his papers in his pocket, 'but I can't promise anything.'

He sat there, smug and fat, looking terribly pleased with himself.

'What's the name of that widow who lives up by there?' he asked. 'She's lost a son in the War.'

'Oh, Margiad Owen, Coedfryn.'

'Yes, that's her. I had to reduce her pension this week.'

Owen and his mother stared at him in astonishment, for they knew Margiad Owen's circumstances well enough to realize that twelve shillings a week was nowhere near enough for her to live on.

'I reduced it from twelve shillings to eight shillings because she keeps hens and was making some money from selling eggs.'

The moment he said that a strange feeling came over Jane Gruffydd. For fifteen months, feelings had been building up inside her against everything responsible for the War, against the men responsible and against God himself; and when she saw this obese man in his sleek clothes rejoicing because he had reduced a poor widow's pension, she could stand it no longer. It was like an abscess bursting: just then this man represented for her everything that was behind the War, and she grabbed the nearest thing to hand – a clothes brush – and struck the official on his head.

'Get out of this house right now,' she said, and he was glad to escape.

'My little boy,' she cried, 'and an old creature like that allowed to live.'

And she and Owen burst out crying together.

25

That same night Owen sat on in the kitchen after his father and mother had gone to bed. He could not think of sleeping because his mind was so agitated. It was almost like the day when the news of Twm's death came. He and his mother had let their feelings sweep over them. Despite that, he felt no better. But instead of thinking only about his brother, now his thoughts went off in all directions. The pensions officer had thrown a stone into a pool, and Owen could not tell where or when the turbulence would end. Before, the loss of his brother had filled the whole compass of his mind and feeling. It was as if the War had been watching their family and had struck Twm down to take revenge on them.

From now on his brother's death would be something hard and cold lying upon his heart, but his mind would be working in other directions. Before this, he had reacted only passively to the War. He suffered some kind of unavoidable fate which had come upon the world, feeling fear and hope; fear that it would come and overwhelm his family, and hope that it would not. In the midst of all this, he saw plenty of kindness mixed with the silly, daft talk. He heard of men getting rich from the War; he saw them from afar. But today he found himself witnessing at first hand a cruel act carried out by one of their people, as it were. Strangely enough, he was not afraid that his mother would be hauled up before the magistrate for hitting the man, and he wasn't worried either if his mother got not a halfpenny of pension, but the sheer cruelty of the thing itself tormented him. That's what war was like; it wasn't only the killing and the suffering that was cruel but casual incidents like this. Like when his mother had to have the news that her son had been killed translated for her.

He broke out in a sweat just thinking of it, and the kitchen became unbearable for him. He lit the lamp, went outside and turned in the direction of the mountain. It was a moonlit night, and the road was greyish white under his feet. A sheep would get up silently from her resting place now and again and run off into the night on hearing his footsteps as he walked past. The sound of the streams was so quiet that it made him think they were simply swirling around in the same spot rather than flowing onward. He sat down on a large rock. The village lay beneath him like fairyland* in the uncanny light of the moon. Here and there like black specks were the houses of the small holdings, with a cluster of trees around them sheltering the yards and buildings. The moon shone on some of the houses, and its light ran in a strip along the roof tiles. The houses' long shadows fell in front of them, and the fields appeared yellow in the moonlight. Right at the bottom was a field of corn in stooks. The earth around where he was sitting was reddish black, and Owen knew that all the land he could see in front of him would have been the same a hundred years before. The people responsible for turning this earth green were by now lying in the parish cemetery, in the richer earth of the plains that lay between him and the sea. Some of them had come from the far ends of the parish to till the soil of the mountain and to live on it, and they went back to their native plot to sleep out the 'long sleep'.

And it wasn't just here in front of his eyes that the work of those hard hands could be seen. He could imagine many countries all over the world, great cities and endless rows of houses roofed with slates from Moel Arian, and the same moon shining down upon them as was throwing down its spears of light on Moel Arian itself tonight.

He turned towards the quarry's waste heap. Tonight it was just a black patch on the side of the mountain. It was the same people who had built farmhouses on the peat land who were responsible for the quarry's waste heap too. Between these two, the villagers had been working hard from morning to night for a hundred years, until they laid down their heads at last before they even reached middle age. Some of them supposed they could help their children avoid this by sending them to Schools and offices and shops.

His thoughts came back to his own family. They were an ordinary example of a family from the district, people who had worked hard, who had had their share of troubles, who had tried to pay their way, though they often failed, and when the end of that was in sight, and there was hope that his parents would have an easier life, here was a totally unexpected blow.

He remembered hearing Ann Ifans say once what smart clothes his mother had when she first came into the district. She never had new clothes now. She bought some mourning clothes when Twm died but she had never worn them since. He remembered how good she had looked that prize-giving day in the County School. In all the family it was only him who tried to help them a bit, though he wasn't the only one who could have done so. He didn't think of that as a virtue on his part. It was softness, nothing more. He couldn't help himself. It was a kind of selfishness. Something had drawn him towards his mother ever since he was a child. He longed to have all her love, but he never got it. He got her kindness and her care, but not her love. He wondered if the other children felt the same way. Except for Elin, home meant nothing to the others. Owen sometimes thought that Twm was closer to his mother's heart than any of the rest of them, but he had no proof of this. Probably she would feel the same if he – Owen – had been lost in the War.

His parents were always reticent about their feelings, and it was difficult to know what gave them pleasure. They enjoyed many things, but he knew for certain that the two of them were looking forward to the day when they were quits with the world and they could enjoy a rest at the end of their lives without having to worry any more. In this they were no different from the rest of the human race. That's what made their bereavement doubly hard, Owen thought. When the prospect of calling it quits with the world was in sight, there came this unexpected blow.

That was what kept drawing him towards his mother and making him try to forget Ann Ellis. Since his foolish love for Gwen years ago, no girl had appealed to him as Ann did. He had not yet fallen head over heels for her, though, but he did like her a lot. At School, he would look forward to the time in the evening when he would be able to talk to her. In his melancholy fit today on his way back from blackberrying, thinking of her was the only ray of hope he had that he would one day feel better. By now, though, the trouble with the pensions officer had changed things again. It wasn't the financial side of things that affected him, but the emotional side. The attraction towards his mother was stronger once more.

And his eyes were opened to the possibility of doing something, instead of suffering mutely. It was high time for someone to stand up against all this injustice. To do something. Thinking about it, that was the trouble with his people. They were heroic in their capacity to suffer, and not in their capacity to do something to oppose the cause of their suffering. William was the only one of his family who had shown opposition to things as they were, unless you could say that Sioned had. Perhaps what she had done was a rebellion against the kind of life her family led, since she lived according to completely different moral standards. Even Twm had turned his back on home and had shown that he could leave it, at any rate. Only he, Owen, was cowardly, that was the truth of the matter. He let his mother hit that pensions officer, when he should have hit him himself. He had never left home, either to go to School or college, without throwing up on account of his homesickness.*

He looked out over the land. Apart from the very faint lights of the town, nobody would have been able to tell that there was a war on anywhere. It was astonishing to think that some little out-of-the-way corner of Wales* like this had a part in the War. And yet, the claws of that beast reached the farthest nooks and crannies of the mountains. A few weeks ago, a lad from the district had deserted from the army and had taken shelter in caves in the rocks, going home to his mother for supper every night. But the army's bloodhounds found him, and he was seen going to the station between two soldiers with a look of defeat upon him. Within three days, the news came that he had been killed in France, and his family and most of the neighbours were gullible enough to believe it. Why didn't the people of the district rise up against something like that? But what was the use of talking? He was one of them himself. He sometimes thought it would have been better if his ancestors had stayed on the other side of Yr Eifl in Lleyn and just carried on tilling the earth.

But perhaps he was, after all, hoping for a life that was too neat, too perfect, and was putting too much trust in the belief that things would turn out right if he did his duty. The webs of people's lives were spread about all over the place, and it was hopeless to think you could draw them neatly together.

He got up from the rock, and saw that there was something familiar about it. He looked more closely and saw that the names of many of the children of the neighbourhood were carved on it, his own name among them. Four of them had been killed in the War. He could see T. G. there clearly, and the letters showed that they were more recent than those of O. G. He remembered that this was the rock they used to rest their bundles of heather on when they used to go and gather it for starting the fire. Then they would haul the bundles up on their backs once more for the final trek down the mountain. As he walked down the same path now, he remembered the smell of the heather and the peat – the heather in the bundle scratching the back of his neck and the particles of earth trickling down under his shirt collar, and his imagination turning the bits of soil into thousands of ants crawling over his skin.

When he reached the house, the cat was sitting on the doorstep. She rubbed herself caressingly against his legs and followed him into the house with her tail up. He turned up the flame in the lamp and gave the fire a poke. The cat kept on rubbing against his legs and purring. He sat in the armchair and reached for his pipe to have a smoke, the first of the day.

A Note on Names and Place Names

Some of the characters in the novel are identified by their first name and the name of their house. This is because of the relative paucity of Welsh surnames: there may be several 'John Ellises' in a district, for example, but only one 'John Twnt i'r Mynydd' (John of Beyond the Mountain). House names are also used to differentiate among members of the same family who have the same name e.g. in the novel, 'Sioned Y Fawnog' is the grandmother, while 'Sioned Ffridd Felen' is the granddaughter. Nevertheless, for the major characters, such as Jane Gruffydd, Kate Roberts tends to use both the first name and surname consistently, somewhat in the manner of Russian novelists endowing their characters with the full complement of names and patronymics. The effect is a dignified one which emphasises the characters' specificity and uniqueness, though Roberts also draws attention to the community's common suffering.

Place names always mean something in Welsh and in this novel they are consistently suggestive of the bleak, rugged terrain in which the characters live out their lives. Most of the place names are fictional but there are also references to actual places in north-west Wales, which fixes the action of the novel in a very particular neighbourhood.

Moel Arian (p. 5 ff.) 'Silver Mountain'. 'Moel' is one of the many words in Welsh for hill or mountain, but it also means 'bald', which tells us what kind of mountain this is. 'Arian' means silver or quicksilver or, indeed, 'money', though the latter is a south Welsh usage primarily. Nevertheless, Roberts might have used it to indicate the money being made by the quarry owners from the slates of this mountain, or to indicate the ironic lack of money suffered by her working characters. Money itself is often a central theme – and bone of contention – in the novel.

Y Fawnog (p. 6 ff.) 'Mawnog' (mutated after the definite article, 'y', to 'fawnog') means 'peat bog' or 'peaty', descriptive of the terrain of this upland landscape.

Lleyn (p. 6 ff.), more often spelled Llŷn, is the Peninsula extending into the Irish sea from the north-west corner of Wales.

Rhyd Garreg (p. 10 ff.) means 'stone ford'.

Ffridd Felen (p. 11 ff.) means 'yellow mountain pasture'.

Waun Goch (p. 17) means 'red moor'.

Allt Eilian (p. 17) means 'Eilian's wood or Eilian's hill'. An 'allt' is a wooded hillside.

Yr Eifl (p. 17 ff.) is a triple-peaked mountain on the Lleyn Peninsula, known in English as 'The Rivals'. Literally, the Welsh word translates as 'the forks'. It is clearly visible from Cae'r Gors, the cottage in Rhosgadfan, Caernarfonshire, where Kate Roberts was born and raised.

Sarn Goch (p. 18 ff.) means 'red causeway'.

Mynydd y Rhiw (p. 20 ff.) means 'mountain slope'. It is an actual mountain near the tip of the Lleyn Peninsula.

Twnt i'r Mynydd (p. 28 ff.) is an oral corruption of 'Tu hwnt i'r Mynydd', meaning 'beyond the mountain'.

Anglesey (p. 46 ff.) – Kate Roberts uses the Welsh

name, 'Sir Fôn', or the county of 'Môn'. The Welsh name derives from Latin, 'Mona' – it was so called by Tacitus and others. After Giraldus Cambrensis, Môn is still frequently called 'mam Cymru', the mother of Wales, on account of its fruitfulness and alleged capacity to feed the whole country. The Gruffydd family's trips to Môn entail a journey from a bleak, upland landscape to gentle, fertile plains. The English name, Anglesey, is Old Norse in origin.

Llanfeuno (p. 46) means 'St Beuno's'. Beuno was a seventh-century saint associated with the Lleyn Peninsula.

Manod (p. 47) means 'snowdrift'. It is also the name of a mountain in north Wales.

Pont Garrog (p. 48) means 'bridge [over the] torrent'.

Cerrig Duon (p. 50) means 'black stones'.

Ceunant (p. 52) means 'gorge' or 'gully'.

Allt Ddu (p. 68) means 'black hill'.

Bron Llech (p. 71 ff.) means 'slate bank'.

Coed y Wern (p. 76) means either 'swamp wood' or 'alder wood'.

Coed Afon (p. 83) means 'river wood'.

Bont y Braich (p. 104) means 'bridge of the arm or ridge'.

Tre Ffrwd (p. 149 ff.) means 'stream town'.

Llan Ddôl (p. 164) means 'church of the meadow'.

Holyhead and Snowdon (p. 173) are the actual places in north Wales; Kate Roberts naturally uses their Welsh names, 'Caergybi' and 'Yr Wyddfa'. 'Caergybi' means 'fort of St Cybi'; Cybi was a sixth-century Celtic saint. 'Yr Wyddfa' means literally 'the mound' or 'tumulus', indicating that it is an ancient burial site. Holyhead is the ferry port for Ireland, which explains the lights 'coming and going' from it.

Meirionethshire (p. 186) is the county in north-west Wales south of Caernarfonshire, where the novel is set. The fact that Ann Ellis is from elsewhere (though only from a neighbouring county) sets her apart somewhat from the rest of the teachers in Llan Ddôl, who are represented as deeply parochial.

Llandudno (p. 193) is a seaside resort on the north Welsh coast. It means 'church of St Tudno'; Tudno was a sixth-century saint.

Bryn Arian (p. 195) means 'silver hill'.

Coed y Ceunant (p. 195) means 'trees of the gully or gorge'. It is a steep-sided, forested valley where Twm goes blackberrying (and where, earlier in the novel, Sioned goes courting). Its secret, sheltered space stands in contrast to the 'bald', almost treeless uplands of Moel Arian.

Coedfryn (p. 198) means 'wooded hill'.

Notes

p. 39 'farthing and a half-farthing': the coins referred to by their Welsh names, 'ffyrling' and 'hadling', were the smallest available denominations at the time. The fact that the difference between a farthing and a half-farthing is a significant one for Jane Gruffydd indicates the family's precarious economic situation. It also emphasizes the importance given to money in Kate Roberts's work, for which some critics condemned her, though she defended herself robustly. She once admitted: 'Mae rhywun wedi deud amdana i mod i'n sôn gormod am arian yn y storïau yma. Nid dyna yn hollol ydi o, ond mae'n rhaid i chi gael arian i fyw, ac mi roedd o'n boen mawr iddyn nhw' (Someone has said about me that I have too much to say about money in these stories. That's not it exactly, but you have to have money to live, and it was a source of great suffering to them [the people of whom she writes]). See: Kate Roberts, Interview with Gwyn Erfyl in *Kate Roberts: Ei Meddwl a'i Gwaith*, ed. Rhydwen Williams (Llandybïe: Christopher Davies, 1983), p. 32.

p. 68 'Disestablishment': that the Anglican church remained the established church in Wales, despite the fact that most Welsh people belonged to the various Nonconformist chapel denominations, was the source of strong discontent in late nineteenth-century Wales. The 'tithe-wars' of the late 1880s were one manifestation of this, when workers in north-east Wales had running battles with police in protest against the legal obligation to pay a tenth (tithe) of their income to a church which they did not frequent. The campaign for Disestablishment of the Anglican church became a national issue and a hotly debated topic. The young Lloyd George was an avid campaigner for Disestablishment; the Act to bring it about was not finally put into effect until 1920.

p.88 'Revival': this refers to the religious revival which swept through the Nonconformist chapels of Wales in 1904-5, led by the charismatic young preacher, Evan Roberts. For a fictionalised account of this phenomenon, see Allen Raine, *Queen of The Rushes* (1906) and Rhys Davies *The Withered Root* (1927).

p. 96 'Thomas Gee and S. R.... Robert Blatchford and Keir Hardie': Thomas Gee (1815-1898) was a hugely influential figure in late nineteenth-century Wales. He founded the publishing company Gee and Sons, along with the newspaper, *Baner ac Amserau Cymru* which Kate Roberts would later edit and publish with her husband from the late 1930s onwards. 'S. R.' was Samuel Roberts (1800-1885) who was also a prominent radical figure in late nineteenth-century Wales. Both of these figures represent the old guard of Welsh cultural and political life. In the early years of the twentieth century these heroes were being ousted by the leaders of the new Labour movement, such as Robert Blatchford (1851-1943), an English socialist campaigner, and Keir Hardie (1856-1915) the Scottish-born politician who was one of the founders of the Labour Party and became the first Labour MP, for Merthyr Tydfil.

p. 98 '1868': The General Election of this year, the first

after the great Reform Act of 1867, saw a decisive shift in Welsh politics, when many Tory MPs lost their seats, and the Liberals under Gladstone became the dominant party in Wales. In some parts of Wales there were reprisals upon and evictions of farmers who had voted for the Liberals instead of for their Tory landlords.

p. 99 'Lloyd George': David Lloyd George (1863-1945) was the Liberal politician brought up in North-West Wales whose meteoric rise to power at the turn of the twentieth century saw him fill key political roles at Westminster, such as Chancellor of the Exchequer (1908-15) and Prime Minister (1916-1922). Initially, Lloyd George was the subject of adulation in Wales, especially as a local hero in the north-west. He was seen as a champion of Home Rule for Wales, of Disestablishment of the Church in Wales, and the hero who brought pensions and national insurance to the poor. But his actions during the First World War dramatically altered the attitudes of many towards him, including Kate Roberts. The fact that he was instrumental in getting the Conscription Act of 1916 passed was one of the many actions that condemned him thoroughly in Roberts's eyes. Her 1923 short story, 'Newid Byd' ('A Change of World') offers a satirical view of Lloyd George, who is nicknamed 'Y Mawr' (the Great One) in the text. Similarly, in Chapter 23 of *Feet in Chains* we are told that the people of Moel Arian started to suspect that 'y bobl fawr' (the big/great people or the bigwigs) were prolonging and profiting from the war.

p. 104 'offrwm': it was a custom in rural Wales for

213

neighbours to make such contributions to a family that had suffered a bereavement, as a token of condolence and as a practical help to cover the costs associated with the funeral. Sometimes the contributions were monetary, sometimes in kind – such as a packet of tea or a bag of sugar. The word 'offrwm' means 'offering' or 'oblation' and has definite religious connotations; the rite is seen as analogous to the 'offering' made regularly in chapel, but it is also indicative of the ethos of mutual help within the community.

p. 114 'swancio': Twm uses a new word which Owen hasn't come across. According to the Oxford English Dictionary, 'to swank', originally a Midlands dialect word, only entered general usage in the early twentieth century. Here, Twm is adapting the new word into Welsh.

p. 115 'Yn iach i ti, Gymru': this is the title of a well-known sentimental and patriotic song by John Ceiriog Hughes (1832-1887).

p. 122 'Nell': Sioned clearly means her sister, Elin, but she is Anglicizing her name, in the same way that Bertie Anglicizes her name from Sioned to 'Janet'.

p. 124 'codi cyn cŵn Caer', literally, 'to get up before the dogs of Chester', is a proverb which translates as having to get up at the crack of dawn. Clearly, the reference is local to north Wales, but the proverb is used all over Wales.

p. 126 'Hwntws': a derogatory term used by people from north Wales to describe those from the south.

p. 131 'Rybela': 'to collect stones from rubble or those rejected or unwanted by quarrymen in "bargains" and turn them into slates', according to Geiriadur Prifysgol Cymru (The University of Wales Dictionary). A 'rybelwr' was a worker who did this; it could be a form of apprenticeship but was also practised by more experienced workers, like William, who did not have a 'bargain' i.e. an agreement which was negotiated monthly with the quarrymen by the steward on behalf of the management. See: R. Merfyn Jones, *The North Wales Quarrymen, 1874–1922* (Cardiff: University of Wales Press, 1981). See also http://www.llechicymru.info/IQTWorkingtheSlate.en glish.html for information about the processes and terminology used in the very specialized and skilful work of the slate quarryman. The discourse of the industry was almost exclusively in Welsh.

p. 131 See R. Merfyn Jones for an account of the complicated negotiations of a 'bargain' at the quarries, which meant that the workmen's wages would often fluctuate dramatically from one month to the next.

p. 137 'Janet': Bertie Anglicizes his wife's name from 'Sioned' to 'Janet'.

p. 142 'mince pies': Sioned uses the English term.

p. 142 *'bara brith'*: literally, 'speckled bread' – a yeasted, cake-like bread with currants or raisins, usually sliced and spread with butter. *Bara brith* is a very homely and traditional Welsh food, with no pretentions, unlike the newfangled 'mince pies' or the expensive 'cake'.

p. 142 'thanciw': Sioned uses the English words, 'thank you', rather than the Welsh word, 'diolch'.

p. 143 'bracelets': Elin's sarcasm is emphasised by her use of the English word.

215

p. 148 '*englyn*': is a four-line verse form in the intricate strict metre tradition of Welsh literature. Its epigrammatic possibilities make it equally suitable for epitaphs or satirical jibes.

p. 158 'Janet': like her son, Mrs Ellis Anglicizes her daughter-in-law's name from Sioned to 'Janet'.

p. 158 'note': Mrs Ellis uses the English word.

p. 158 'suspicious': Mrs Ellis uses the English word.

p. 160 and p. 176 'first growth of grass': Kate Roberts calls this 'gwellt medi' (harvest grass) and adds an endnote to explain that this was the term used to describe the thick growth of grass which springs up around muckheaps or drains; it was harvested first in the summer and fed to the animals while still green.

p. 160 'wedi mynd rhwng y cŵn a'r brain, a'r rhai hynny yn gŵn a brain estron hefyd': literally, 'gone among the dogs and the crows, and foreign dogs and crows, too'. For something to go 'among the dogs and the crows' in Welsh means for it to be utterly lost or ruined. The phrase is proverbial but Ifan seems to be turning it over bitterly in his mind and associating Bertie with the alien 'dogs and crows'.

p. 173 '*cywydd*': a Welsh strict metre verse form consisting of rhyming couplets of seven-syllable lines with intricate alliteration. It is a much longer form than the *englyn*; its greatest exponent was the fourteenth-century poet, Dafydd ap Gwilym.

p. 177 'Now' is Twm's affectionate nickname for his brother, Owen.

p. 180 'corn carw', literally 'stag's horn'. This is the plant 'lycopodiella inundata' which in English is called marsh clubmoss. It is a typical plant in upland Snowdonia.

p. 181 This couplet is from a work by the sixteenth-century
poet, Siôn Tudur. Twm is 'using his knowledge of Welsh' in his letter to Owen, something which he has not been able to do professionally, to his frustration.

p. 191 'mi rôi garreg ar ei faw, tae o'n medru', literally, 'he'd put a stone on his shit, if he could'. Ann Ifans, despite the depths of her grief, is still capable of coming up with a suitably rude description of her son's former boss.

p. 193 'ice cream': Eric uses the English words.

p. 195 and p. 203 'hiraeth' in Welsh. This word often remains untranslated and, arguably, cannot be translated exactly. It often means homesickness, as it does when Owen dreads leaving home (p. 81) but at other times it is a deep feeling of loss, regret or nostalgia. Compare German *Sehnsucht* and Portuguese *saudade*.

p. 200 'gwlad y Tylwyth Teg', literally, 'the land of the fair relatives'. Fairies and other supernatural beings are called the 'tylwyth teg' in Welsh, indicating that they are kin to humans but more beautiful.

p. 203 'Wales': this is one of the few times in the novel that Wales is actually named. It indicates a growing political consciousness in Owen and an ability to see his own family in an historical, social, and national context.

Katie Gramich is a Professor of English Literature at Cardiff University. A specialist in the literature of modern Wales and in rediscovering neglected Welsh women writers, she has served as Chair of the Association for Welsh Writing in English and edits the *Almanac* series.

The best new research by established
and emerging critics in the field of
Welsh writing in English

Volume 16   £14.99   ISBN 9781908069931

Volume 16 continues its commitment to publishing the best new research. Topics discussed include revolutionary poetry, the politics of translation, the forging of the canon of Welsh writing in English, and the peculiarities of Welsh Modernism, with the indispensible annual critical bibliography, complied by Emma Schofield.

Contrasting essays provide fresh insight into the work of Caradoc Evans; four essays examine very diverse poetry; the politics and practice of translation in Wales are incisively surveyed; and attention is focused on the fascinating Russian translation of classic 1880 novel, *The Rebecca Rioter*.

www.parthianbooks.com

'Setting a new agenda and a new standard for literary criticism in Wales.' Professor Dafydd Johnston

Volume 15
£14.99
ISBN 9781906998431

Volume 14
£14.99
ISBN 9781906998318

Volume 13
£14.99
ISBN 9781905762781

Volume 12
£14.99
ISBN 9781905762750

www.parthianbooks.com

LIBRARY OF WALES

New Titles

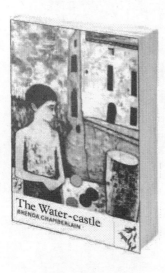

£8.99 ISBN 9781908069795

The Water-castle is a journal of love and discord in post-war Germany as a Welsh woman travels with her French husband to meet her former lover, a German count.

£8.99 ISBN 9781908069795

Lovers Rees Stevens and Ellen Vaughan, must discover and interpret Ellen's father's journal if all the fires of living on are not to fall into cold ash. Ron Berry's masterpiece covers the kaleidoscopic history of the South Wales valleys.

www.thelibraryofwales.com

£20.00 Limited Edition Hardback
ISBN 9781908069757
£9.99 Paperback
ISBN 9781908069726

'The descriptive passages remind one what a splendid poet the author is.' *Observer*

Incorporates Dannie's acclaimed first volume of autobiography, *A Poet in the Family*, and brings his life up to the present and the outset of a new century.

£9.99 ISBN 9781908069719

'Every reader of the *The Volunteers* can testify to its power and pace as a detective thriller.' *Tony Pinkey*

A striking worker is killed; a minister is shot. Lewis Redfern pursues the killer, through a maze of government leaks and international politics to secret organization the Volunteers.

£8.99 ISBN 9781908069733

'Encountering reality and the tragic elements of dream...a remarkable achievement.' *New York Times*

As the newly-built foundries of 1830s South Wales enter their first decline, a travelling harpist from the rural north arrives in one of the new towns to find his friends caught in a fiercely-fought industrial dispute which quickly spirals out of control.

www.thelibraryofwales.com

PARTHIAN   Fiction

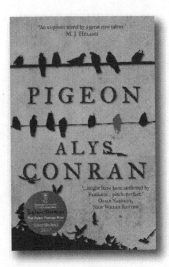

Pigeon

Alys Conran
ISBN 978-1-910901-23-6
£8.99 • Paperback

Winner of Wales Book of the Year
Winner of Rhys Davies Award

'An exquisite novel by a great new talent.' – M.J. Hyland

Ironopolis

Glen James Brown
ISBN 978-1-912681-09-9
£9.99 • Paperback

Shortlisted for the Orwell Prize for Political Fiction

'A triumph' – *The Guardian*

'The most accomplished working-class novel of the last few years.' – *Morning Star*

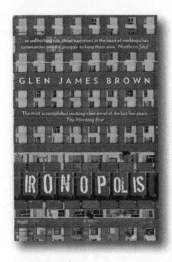

PARTHIAN　　Fiction

The Levels

Helen Pendry
ISBN 978-1-912109-40-1
£8.99 • Paperback

'...an important new literary voice.'
– Wales Arts Review

Shattercone

Tristan Hughes
ISBN 978-1-912681-47-1
£8.99 • Paperback

On *Hummingbird*:
'Superbly accomplished... Hughes prose is
startling and luminous' – *Financial Times*

Hello Friend
We Missed You

Richard Owain Roberts
ISBN 978-1-912681-49-5
£9.99 • Paperback

'The Welsh David Foster Wallace'
– Srdjan Srdic

The Blue Tent

Richard Gwyn
ISBN 978-1-912681-28-0
£10 • Paperback

'One of the most satisfying, engrossing and
perfectly realised novels of the year.'
– *The Western Mail*